Metaphorosis

September 2023

Beautifully made speculative fiction

Also from Metaphorosis

<u>Metaphorosis Magazine</u>

Metaphorosis: Best of 20xx
Metaphorosis 20xx: The Complete Stories
annual issues, from 2016
Monthly issues

<u>Plant Based Press</u>

Best Vegan Science Fiction & Fantasy
annual issues, 2016-2020

from B. Morris Allen:
Chambers of the Heart: speculative stories
Susurrus
Allenthology: Volume I
Tocsin: and other stories
Start with Stones: collected stories
Metaphorosis: a collection of stories

<u>Verdage</u>

Reading 5X5 x3: Changes
Reading 5X5 x2: Duets
Score: an SFF symphony
Reading 5X5: Readers' Edition
Reading 5X5: Writers' Edition

<u>Vestige</u>

The Nocturnals, by Mariah Montoya

<u>Joyful Heave</u>

Museum Piece: an unusual collection

Metaphorosis

September 2023

edited by
B. Morris Allen

ISSN: 2573-136X (online)
ISBN: 978-1-64076-265-7 (e-book)
ISBN: 978-1-64076-266-4 (paperback)

Metaphorosis
a magazine of speculative fiction

from
Metaphorosis Publishing

Neskowin

September 2023

That Lonesome, Restless Feeling

B. Morris Allen

Outside the house, a placard swung slightly in the twilight breeze. To and fro, to and fro, never making any progress as it moved in complex helices at hundreds of meters per second through the solar system, or hundreds of kilometers per second through the galaxy. Motion was a matter of perspective.

The house had never moved. It stood where it always had, where it had stood throughout their marriage. It would never move, until the great Northwest earthquake finally came and flung it toward the Pacific. Then, at last, the closets would open, the drawers would break, and there would be chaos until the tsunami came and washed it all clean.

It had always been clean, of course. Always spotless, always ordered, always neat, until she returned from a trip with her dusty luggage, her tacky gifts, her long-winded stories. Madhup had cleaned them up, labeled them, put them away for future use. Madhup had always known where they were, what they were for, when they'd last been touched. And she, Bettina, had relied on that, let her own memory atrophy. She'd wiped it clean with every arrival, left it empty to be filled again, on her next trip out to Centauri, or Aldebaran, or some unnamed new system, with unnamed new planets.

She'd left her memories here, in this dark house, on the grey Oregon coast, stored away with bookends and croquet sets and nameless artifacts. Madhup had stored them, kept them, known that without them, Bettina was not Bettina, was not the galactic traveller, the intrepid explorer, the feted hero.

"Without you, I'm nothing," she whispered to the gloom of the hallway. It was hardly a room at all — just a wide space where real rooms came together. The stairs to the dormitory, seldom used;

the doors to the laundry, the guest bath, the library, the guest room. Grand names for empty spaces. And this plain hallway, with its entries and exits and its shallow linen closet. Hardly a room at all. And yet it had a ghost.

"You always were thorough, Madhup." After the funeral, when she'd unpacked, when she'd had time to look around, when she'd looked for something to fill her time, she'd found the folder, neatly labeled, in the middle of the library desk. Doctors, crematoria, wills, accounts, utilities, passwords. Everything was there. Everything but Madhup. For that, there were the ghosts.

She hadn't seen them, at first. She'd stared down at the folder, watching it blur and blur until the ocean broke her walls and spilled out all over the neat, printed label, turning 'After death' into a confusing, smudgy mess of ink and paper.

She'd cried and cried, curled into a corner of the tiny library, face pressed into the books until she realized she was pushing them out of line, and then turned the other way and cried some more. When at last the sea was empty, her heart wrung tight until it hurt, she let it go, let it curl like a wounded animal in the cage of her chest, wanting and fearing to be free. That was when she'd seen the ghost.

It wasn't ghostly. It was Madhup, solid, stolid, serious. Working with her files, with a softscreen hung from the windowsill, a keyboard at her fingertips. Spreadsheets, documents, investments — dull things, important things. She didn't moan or shake or turn to mist. She didn't look up, not even when Bettina scrambled to her feet, launched herself bodily at her wife, scrabbling, grabbing, gabbling.

"You're not... you're here... you're alive!" But of course she wasn't. She was a hint of ashes spread across the beach, blown into the surf, eaten by molecrabs or sand hoppers.

And yet, she'd sat there, solid, unmovable, typing her figures, scrolling her documents. Dutiful and unresponsive. Lost in her own world, as she had liked to say, 'without even leaving the house.'

Bettina had sat there for hours, watching, holding, feeling Madhup's dead heartbeat. She'd cajoled, entreated, threatened. She'd tried to take the keyboard, to stop the fingers, but ghosts were stronger than hope, it seemed. They played by their own rules.

She'd stayed for days, taking catnaps on the floor, or on the desk itself, half-curled on the corner still available. Frightened at every waking that Madhup would be gone again, and she'd be alone for real. But always the ghost was there, still typing, still working. It wasn't a loop, that she could see. Not a creation of the holojector she'd brought back from Tarsis IV as her first big find, the one that had bought them the house, paid off the loans, let Madhup do her research, Bettina her exploring.

Ghost Madhup did different things, used different files. But they were old, irrelevant. They said nothing to Bettina. Most of them she barely recognized. It was not until the second day that she noticed, finally looked carefully at the softscreen. At the upper right, a small icon — a little blob of text. The ghost never touched it, never tapped it. But the space was always clear; however the windows and desktops shifted, that one little icon was never covered.

The workspace was still there, of course, still stored on their little server, its passcodes carefully spelled out in Madhup's perfect, awful folder. Bettina pulled her glasscreens from her pocket, settled them on her nose, logged in. The desktop was bare, clean, save for one little icon. It did nothing when she tapped it, had no hidden information in the properties. At last, she zoomed the screen, and then she got it. It was just an icon, a tiny image of black text on white — a poem Bettina had written for Madhup, back when she'd thought she was an artist. It had been terrible — painful, hackneyed promises of love they'd both laughed about, agreeing that maybe Bettina should stick to exploring and adventure — the things that she was good at.

She'd cried a little more, then, but only a little. There were only so many tears a body could make, so much emotion a soul could take. She'd hugged the ghost again, and staggered out to fall asleep on the soft covers of the guest bed — always fresh, never musty, seldom used.

When she woke, the ghost was there. A younger ghost, a younger Madhup. A little chubbier, a little less grey, a little less certain. She stood in the doorway, looking in at the bed. She smiled, she shrugged, she flirted. She laughed, all soundless. She looked happy, then troubled, then happy again. And in her eyes, a hunger seemed to burn, that made her look lost and brave and vulnerable all at once.

Bettina had lain in bed and smiled, waved. Basked in this memory of the younger Madhup. Had called her over, knowing that the ghost would not respond, could not respond, that these were passive ghosts, for all they moved and acted. And despite entreaties and enticements, ghost Madhup never left the doorway, only glancing away from time to time when the troubled looks came across her brow.

After a while, Bettina had gotten up, stood next to the ghost, hugged it. It felt warm, comforting. It was just like the real Madhup. It was Madhup, it seemed, when she'd been younger. From close up, she could see the lack of grey, the fainter wrinkles. Five years ago, maybe seven. Bettina had been gone a lot, then. She'd been exploring around Rigel, had always been on the point of the next big find, in promising ruins that turned out to be natural crystal formations, or in deep caverns that held nothing but ice. She'd barely been home at all, for about two years. They'd talked via long videos back and forth through courier bots. Madhup had never complained, never said how lonely she was, though Bettina had seen it in her eyes.

She'd realized then, standing next to the ghost, what she should have seen at first. It wasn't Bettina the ghost was looking at. Why would it be, lying in the guest bed? She'd never slept there, until today. It was a guest, of course. A guest who'd flirted, cajoled, entreated. A Madhup who'd laughed and giggled, and felt guilty.

Bettina had been angry then, confused. She hadn't known. Couldn't remember who'd visited then, or whether anyone had. That was Madhup's department, all the social arrangements, the friends, the schedules. Bettina's job was to find things, Madhup's in part to put them in their places.

She'd been alone. For years at a time, sometimes.

"But you never complained!" And why should she have? That was the way things were, the rules laid out by Bettina, the active one, the famous one, the one who got her way.

She sat on the bed, got up again, feeling the invisible, intangible presence of the other ghost, the one ghost-Madhup was winking at.

"Why this? Why show me this? Why save *this*?" For there was no doubt Madhup had done this, had selected these memories, had arranged her own haunting somehow.

Bettina turned to leave, to go… somewhere, to think. And yet, as she came to the door, to the sly, leering, potentially unfaithful Madhup, she paused. For this was Madhup too. This was her, and what she'd done, and what she'd felt. It was honest, as Madhup had always been honest. Even after death, when her ghost itself was an illusion, she was honest.

The ghost was always in the doorway. Just on the threshold. It never came inside. Never sat, and smiled a sultry smile, never ran a gentle hand along the leg that wasn't there. It burned with passion, but it burned alone.

That was the message, she supposed, and it was true. She'd left Madhup alone, and trusted her. She, out among the stars, with a ship and its robots as companions, had been focused on her work. It had never occurred to her that Madhup, alone among temptations, might feel lonely. Not in a real way. They'd talked about it, joked about it, but it had never really sunk beneath the surface of her mind. Yet it had happened. And Madhup had acted on it, or she had not. Either way, Bettina had contributed. And either way, it didn't really matter. What mattered was that there had been more to Madhup than she'd known, more than she had ever thought to explore.

She'd stumbled out to the kitchen, hungry and confused, and hurt by her own actions and inaction. There was food, of course, tidily labeled containers of frozen food she'd cooked herself, and that Madhup had divided and packaged and put away.

It had always surprised people, that Bettina was the one who cooked. 'I thought you were the' this type or that type, they liked to say. People liked to label things. Like Madhup, she admitted. Madhup had liked to label things, to organize them, to put them into boxes.

Her ghost sat now, on her little stool beside the pantry, where she'd always sat while Bettina cooked, marking pen in hand, wet wipe in the other. As Bettina's meal defrosted, ghost Madhup labeled and packed, sorted and cleaned. She wrote new labels on in her terrible handwriting, wiped old ones off with her little cloth, so that smudges of ink always got on her fingers, and they looked liked she'd contracted some dread disease.

'Something you brought back from Zubenelgenubi,' she always said, because she liked the name so much, couldn't believe it was a real star. 'A deadly alien virus from one of your gadgets.'

Because the gadgets weren't always obvious. They usually weren't. There were only a few that Bettina had immediately understood, had seen the use of, once she'd, via robot, pushed all the buttons, pulled all the levers. Most of them, she brought home to Madhup, to classify and test and send to experts. That was where most of the money came from — the little day-to-day sums that paid for the food, the utilities, the fuel for Bettina's ship, the lawyers to make sure the rights were locked down. She'd have to manage that on her own, now, or hire someone to do it. There would be names in Madhup's folder, a plan, step-by-step directions.

She ate in the kitchen, from an immaculate little bowl, a bean curd lasagna that she'd made weeks ago, before another trip, before she'd known about the cancer.

She watched ghost Madhup label spices and cereals, little plastic containers of frozen goulasch, big bags of alien gimcrack. For a while, she sat against her dead lover's knees, telling her all the stories again.

"I found that one in a city of broken crystal spheres. I cut my suit open, but I got a patch on in time. The city was all smashed into shards and powder, but it was beautiful, with the light from a blue sun refracting through the bits and throwing rainbows everywhere.

"That one was from a little satellite out in the middle of nowhere. It's incredible I found it; there was no system there at all, just a ring of dust with a radius of about 10 AUs. The satellite was right in the middle, right where a star should have been. Not really a satellite so much as a three dimensional metal frame, really. I felt bad about taking it, after. Maybe it was just a monument, or a piece of art.

"This one was from the same sector where I found the holojector, about 32 light years away. I thought at first it was the same folks — see how it has sort of that same filigreed cylinder look? But I could never figure out how it worked, so maybe it was someone else's.

"Ooh, that one. You remember that one, you got it working. The molecular needle, you called it, cause it makes stitches so small, and out of anything. You said it pays the property tax.

"This one..." She talked and talked, and ate again when the ghost moved back to foods and rolls of tape and carefully sorted cables. It looked happy, or at least content. Had it sat there, had Madhup sat there when Bettina wasn't home? Had she done familiar things to pretend Bettina was there, or had she had some other life, with different habits, different places? Whichever this was a memory of, it wasn't unhappy. That was enough.

She slept that night in the master bedroom, with its French doors open to the sound of waves, and the fog floating in through the screen. She curled around the warm, solid figure of Madhup's ghost, in its camisole and garish, ludicrous pajama pants. It felt alive. Its heart beat, its lungs breathed, it fidgeted. Mostly, though, it slept, and it snuggled. Sometimes in the back, curled up to face Bettina, so that she could lie facing its closed eyes and slightly smiling face, ghostly in the moonlight, or push herself back against it and imagine that its other arm wound around her, crossed between her breasts so that she could kiss it as she slept. Mostly it lay the other way, and Betting curled around its question mark shape, spooned like big dipper and small. 'Always with the astronomy,' Madhup had complained. But she'd come out to lie on the beach with Bettina anyway, to look where she pointed and to ooh and aah about invisibly distant stars she would never visit.

'I'm happy where I am,' she'd said. She'd visited Bettina's ship, the Lightfoot, one time. 'It's so cramped,' she'd said. 'And so … plain.' As if a scoutship had room or mass for decorations and luxury. 'I need my beach and my eagles, and my garden, and my deer. I need seals, nasturtiums, whales, bluejays, crows, garlic, sand, surf, blackberries, rain.' All of which were right here, outside the house and sometimes in it. She fell asleep with her face deep in ghost hair, her hand tight against soft ghost belly. It was still there when she woke.

She ate pancakes with the cataloging ghost, shaking pancake mix from a labeled container, dropping in frozen huckleberries from the garden. She didn't tell any stories as alien artifacts passed through dead hands, only watched as they were slid into padded containers and labeled with scrawled but detailed notes, due to be replaced later with machine printed ones that a person could actually read. When the ghost started packing fresh blueberries into plastic freezer containers, she kissed it on the head, and went to wash.

The bathroom was a horror. In the tub, chest deep in steaming water, a wasted ghost shivered as it wiped loose grey hairs from its mottled scalp, and set them apologetically on the rim. It smiled, a horrific rictus of thin lips and skin, and held its bony hand out for help. Dripping wet, it staggered out two steps to the toilet, and retched and retched and retched, until the water was pink and the bowl streaked with crimson.

Bettina held the ghost Madhup's hair, what was left of it, and wiped its face clean while she cried. It looked at her with a depth of devotion so absolute that she felt her heart begin to tear within her chest. She left before it came completely loose of its stitches.

She showered in the guest bath, whose ghost did nothing worse than brush healthy gums and draw little hearts on the steamed-up glass with M + B inside. She avoided it and left to sit on the master bed. Beside her, a healthy dead woman slumbered and drooled a bit from a slightly open mouth.

After half an hour of blankness, her mind empty of coherent thought, she was no further along. With a trepidation that bordered almost on fear, she went back to the bathroom to face her memories.

For hours, she bathed the ghost, and held its hair, and wiped its face, and helped it stand and sit, in a long and painful cycle with no defined start or end. It washed and dried, and vomited and defecated, all with a look of gratitude and love that broke her heart over and over and over, until she felt there was nothing left but dust.

It was the most painful of memories, brought back from the dead, condensed to relive as often as she could stand. She stood it until evening, alternating bouts of guilt with anger and despair.

She left again for dinner, some nameless stew of lentils and vegetables that Madhup herself had made. It was solid, filling, flavorless. She ate it in the living room, where Madhup sat reading and watching birds out the window and feeding the non-existent fire, just as she had in life.

When the stew was done, she did the dishes, wiping the marker notes off the plastic stew container with careful hands that trembled as she prepared herself for the bathroom again.

That was why she was here, it was clear. That was how she was haunted, how at last the ghost followed classic rules of fear and horror and disgust. Disgust with herself, for leaving Madhup alone, for failing her. Fear at the future before her, of an endless round comforting an eternally dying ghost. Expiating her guilt for as long as she lived, or worse, as long as she could stand it until she left and built up more guilt, more moral debt.

The bathroom ghost smiled its familiar, fragile smile at Bettina's invisible past. She remembered this one, she found — this particular smile, this particular moment, so recent, so painful. They'd come back from a trip to the beach. Walking slowly, the wheelchair disdained for this one last excursion. 'Our last exploration together,' Madhup had said, and Bettina had denied it, pretending there would be many more, knowing Madhup would die that night, or the next one. It had been three nights. Three days cooking elaborate purees of this and that when Madhup was sleeping after vomiting up the last one. Three days spent sitting just here, on the edge of the tub, holding her hair and bathing her sunken frame.

She started to recall the other smiles, the other gestures, the other looks. She remembered them all, made a puzzle of placing them all in context, nicely labeled the way Madhup would have liked it. She fell asleep by the side of the tub, holding the ghost's frail hand.

The cycle was still going when she woke up. This was from the day before Madhup's death, when she was so weak Bettina had had to carry her in to the toilet and the tub, had had to change the sheets. And all through it, Madhup had smiled and joked. She was making one now, Bettina saw.

'Let m stand for an unknown,' Bettina mouthed with her. 'No, we need something bigger. We'll use n.' It was Madhup's favorite joke, a relic from her days as a mathematician. She'd told it that day just to see Bettina roll her eyes. Bettina remembered doing it.

That was the point, she realized. She remembered all these moments. She'd been there. She'd held the hand, wiped the bottom, cleaned the hair from the rim of the tub. That was Madhup's message. Not 'I died and it's your fault,' because it wasn't. It was cancer's fault. Madhup was saying instead, 'I died and you were here for me. I died and you took care of me. I died in your arms, and I was happy. Don't forget this. Don't block it out. It was important to me, and it's important to you.'

Maybe it was wishful thinking. Maybe Madhup was a classic vindictive ghost. But only if dying made you a different person. She chuckled through the tears. That was a joke Madhup would have liked.

"Only if dying makes you a different person," she said, and the ghost held out her hand for help getting up.

The next morning, she woke early. She had breakfast with a silent ghost, then went upstairs to the dormitory. As she had expected, it was full of Madhup. Madhup rolling around, racing, turning somersaults among the beds. Madhup playing with the nieces and nephews, with borrowed dogs and cats to which Bettina was allergic. The ghost laughed its silent, exuberant laugh, played peek-a-boo with babies, board games with youngsters, sat silent and comforting with teenagers, napped on the sunlit floor with cats on her legs and dog heads on her chest.

And now the hallway, at the base of those tall steps, with the irregular one painted orange, at the confluence of doors and travel. And here, in the shadowed gloom, was one more ghost. Madhup, in middle age, in the comfortable jeans and cotton blouse that made her look a little dumpy, with her arms out waiting to be hugged.

She hugged and was hugged, kissed and was kissed, looked into small brown eyes that looked into hers. Remembered and was, perhaps, somewhere, remembered. Loved and was loved in precious memory.

She'd made the calls this morning, and the agent from Madhup's folder had put up the sign that afternoon. She could just see it from here, through the glass of the front door, swinging aimlessly in its circular, spiral voyage that went nowhere at vast speeds around the galaxy.

She knew now, what she'd find in the laundry room. No shelves of carefully cataloged mysteries. They would have been packaged up, sold, donated. There would be an intent, happy ghost, doing the work she loved the best — putting together puzzles, solving problems in her little workshop. And on a desk or a workbench would be a little filigreed cylinder that was like her holojector after all, that somehow made memory solid, or made the past solid, or something. A device that Madhup had figured out, a puzzle she had solved. Just as she had solved the puzzle of what to do with Bettina's grief, how to hold her wife's hand even after death, how to bring her through the grief and guilt and the 'if I had only' moments to give Madhup the credit she deserved, to remember that it had been a partnership, and they had both had what they wanted most, and had paid a price.

"It was worth it," Bettina said as she found the cylinder, read the careful directions, and twisted it just so. "It was worth every minute," as she put the cylinder back and a ghost slowly faded out of sight. And though tears rolled down her cheeks, for the first time in weeks, her heart beat free in her chest.

She'd walked through the empty house, left the door unlocked behind her. She would go out again, into the night, to lose that lonesome, restless feeling in the space between the stars. She'd go further than she'd ever gone — exploring, as she'd always done, in her cramped, plain little ship, with only memory for company.

See B. Morris Allen's story "That Lonesome, Restless Feeling" online at Metaphorosis.
If you liked it, leave a comment. Authors love that!
Remember to subscribe to our e-mail updates so you'll know when new stories are posted.

About the story

Many of my stories are sparked by song lyrics — whether or not correctly heard. In this case, I'm fairly confident I got them right, and the story draws on Gordon Lightfoot's song, "Ordinary Man". I'm not usually drawn to ghost stories, but I liked the line about "a ghost in every room", and, since I write SFF, made it a science fiction ghost created by an alien artifact. The ending draws on a lyric that's a little less obvious — a line from Herbert Grönemeyer's beautiful song, "Der Weg", about going on ("Hab' meine Frist verlängert") even in the face of tragedy.

Arborify

Cadence Mandybura

Bang.

Yvonne flinched at the pop of the anti-drone cannon. She rushed to the nearest tree, placed her hand against the papery bark, whispered, "It's okay." In the past seventeen seasons of working at the arborification facility, Yvonne had typically only heard the cannons go off once or twice a year. Now they sounded at least a dozen times a day.

She caught one of her subordinates staring at her as he walked past, but he flicked his gaze downward immediately. Yvonne narrowed her eyes as he quickened his pace away from her. From her co-workers' perspective, the drones weren't dangerous, just Shut It Down fanatics angling to get footage of the arborification process, looking for abuses that didn't exist. But the trees didn't know that, and the violence of the cannon noise might be distressing to them. Yvonne comforted them where she could.

Her colleagues were only worried about the safety of their pension-clad jobs. That fear was too big to be sharp for Yvonne; imagining life without this career was an ungraspable blankness. She had been eight when Ms. Moyo had explained to her that the birch trees outside the big kids' entrance were from the government's arborification tree-planting program, and so some of them might have once been people. When navigating playground friendships became too difficult, Yvonne would retreat to the trees, wishing she could root herself more fully to their calm presence. It felt safe to her, that people could become trees; that the chaos and questions and pain of life could be quieted into the simplicity of sunlight and sap.

Another cannon boom, a whipcrack echo.

Yvonne winced, moved to another tree in the grove to murmur reassurances.

Inside, she cursed Malcolmson, that young thug, for being the first to attack the trees, for inspiring the Shut It Downers, but she didn't want her charges hearing her anger. This batch was about six weeks old. Planted to mid-calf, with their linen clothing starting to melt into bark, their human faces were still recognizable, but with clear signs that arborification was underway: the thinning lips, flattened ears, and eyebrows tugged away by the wind.

She walked among the trees, checking for parasites or other signs that growth wasn't progressing normally. She noticed, weightlessly, the marks of the trees' former lives. Many had tattoos, some of them gang markers in cheap prison ink; one tree had needle scars on its forearm; another had suicide attempts racked into its wrists. Most, though, were just old, frail creatures, now at peace, alchemizing light, water, and air.

"Hello, my friend," said Yvonne to one of them. "Don't be afraid of the noise. You're safe here." A bulb of amber liquid glimmered at the corner of the tree's left eye. Yvonne dabbed it away; the eyelid fluttered at the contact, a reflex to be expected at this early stage. Yvonne still had a print on her wall that she had bought as a teenager: a famous photo of the weeping trees. The work of a muckraking journalist back in the early days of arborification, the image had sparked the first wave of protests. The scientific community had done its best to quell the outrage with beige reassurances. There was no evidence of consciousness at the weeping stage. All clients gave their full consent prior to the procedure. Within minutes of the injections, all human brain activity ceased. The occasional blinking and lip twitches were automatic gestures that faded as the clients' anatomy transformed.

Public opinion hadn't truly swung until a pop megastar announced her choice to arborify at the end of her struggle with ovarian cancer. Other celebrities took up the cause, championing arborification as a compassionate and sustainable process. Today, people were content with the status quo, mostly ignoring a government program that, over decades, had quietly eased the strain on social systems. Some outrage remained, but it had narrowed to the margins.

Until Malcolmson. Yvonne squeezed her eyes shut, bit her lip until she cut through to the salt-iron of blood.

Yvonne could still see the news reports from the event, forty-one days ago: yellow hazard tape flapping at the edge of a stand of birch. At least two trees fully felled, others gashed and keeling over in pain. A close-up of the stumps, the broken trunks splattered with a rust-brown liquid. Yvonne's first thought had been of cough syrup, the gross, medicinal kind. It had turned out to be cow's blood.

And the kid behind it: Rawling Malcolmson, legally an adult at eighteen, but still in high school. Revulsion had slithered through Yvonne as she consumed his features: smirking, even though it was a mugshot, smirking for god's sake. His tight cap of dark hair started far down the nape of his neck, creeping to a widow's peak that skewed left. His face was shiny and thin, spotted with a few pimples, with wide-set slug-coloured eyes.

He had been easily caught and didn't have anything to say; he clammed up on the advice of his lawyers and everyone was still waiting for the gears of justice to establish his guilt and pass sentence.

Just another maladjusted youth, some speculated, lashing out for attention. Others saw him as the forefront of a renewed campaign against arborification. Yvonne didn't know which was true. She hated him regardless.

Yvonne's watch buzzed. Town hall in ten minutes. Reluctantly, she left the grove and followed the dirt path through the fields back to the main building. As always, her hand drifted up from her side, finger pads towards the trees, as she repeated her usual silent greeting.

Hello. Hello, my friend. Hello.

" 'Dear class,' " the substitute begins in her scratchy voice. Yvonne hates going to school now, but today's a good day. Today they get to hear another letter from their teacher, Ms. Moyo, who's been gone on medical leave since February but has written a letter to the class every week during her absence. Yvonne sits at the back edge of the classroom carpet, scratches even-branched Ys onto her frayed corduroys, not sure why her stomach is twisting so much. She

desperately wants to hear the letter. She also doesn't.

" 'This will be my last letter to you,' " the substitute continues. Yvonne freezes. Her face becomes a knot, her throat and chest, too, as the tangle of her emotions cinch tight.

She sobs. Too loud. Frankie O imitates her, his friends giggle. Yvonne covers her face.

The substitute clears her throat starchily; the boys quiet down. She continues Ms. Moyo's letter to the class.

" 'This is my last letter to you, but I'm not going away forever, and at the end of this letter I'll tell you how we can stay in touch.' "

Yvonne's darkness sprays with shapes as her palms press into her eyes. She sniffs, puts her hands back in her lap, and listens hard.

Town halls were bullshit. The deputy minister's office had only started hosting them when people began quitting because of the Shut It Down harassment. After the initial Malcolmson incident, when it still seemed like an isolated case? Nothing.

Yvonne tucked herself into a corner carrel, plugged in the headset, and fished out a notepad from the top drawer. She doodled as the meeting got underway. It helped to scratch out her frustration.

Today's town hall was about the increase in drones. First, an assurance of their safety—the military had set up additional cannons and radar, not even a horsefly could get through, hur hur—but the meeting soon morphed to offers of transfers, temporary leave, psychological support. Blah, blah, blah. The deputy minister had no good answers for how the division would take care of the trees with a reduced workforce. Yvonne fractalized the heavy Y she had drawn into the pad, repeating the pattern in smaller increments.

During the Q&A, people asked what would happen to their jobs if the facility shut down. The deputy minister didn't seem to think of it as a real threat; the protests were loud, he acknowledged, but the silent majority was content with arborification. Everyone knew it had been one of the greatest successes of the past century, addressing challenges in health care, homelessness, addiction, and the environment all at the same time. Still, if the facility closed, employees would be offered positions elsewhere within government. No one would be left out in the cold.

Except for the clients, Yvonne wanted to say, jerking her drawing to a stop as her pen ripped a furrow in the paper. Without arborification, where would they go?

Halfway through Ms. Moyo's letter, Naima raises her hand. "I thought only bad people were borified," she says.

"Arborified," the substitute corrects quickly; Yvonne does the same under her breath. "Who told you that?"

Naima shrugs. "Like, it's for criminals and stuff."

"Whoa, wait, is Ms. Moyo in jail?" says Frankie O. Yvonne wants to hit him, but he's too far away.

"No, no. Ms. Moyo is very, very sick," the substitute says, glaring at Frankie, before turning back to Naima. "There are people in our justice system who sometimes choose to become arborified. That might be what you're thinking of. But it has nothing to do with being good or bad.

It's just an option for people who are ready for a different sort of life."

Naima looks uncertain. "So… Ms. Moyo… because she's so sick…"

The substitute nods. "Incurable," she says. "It's quite common for people in her predicament. Yes, Ricardo? Speak up."

Ricardo's a shy boy; Yvonne was friends with him for part of first grade until he got mad at her for borrowing his toque without asking. She was going to give it back, but he didn't understand when she tried to explain. Now, whenever she looks at him, she has an ugly, bubbly feeling, even when he's being nice.

"Are the doctors making Ms. Moyo arborify?" he asks now.

"Of course not. It's always a choice. This is what she wants. In fact, if we keep reading, the next sentence says, 'I know this may seem sad, my young friends, but I want you to know that this is not an end, just a transformation…' "

Yvonne looks away from Ricardo, thinks of Ms. Moyo instead, her soft nose, her big laugh, her bright lipstick. Of course, Ms. Moyo wouldn't just end. She wouldn't do that to Yvonne.

"Shut! It! Down!"

Yvonne hid her head between her knees as her car glided past the perimeter fence. There had always been a few tired protestors at the edge of the arborification grounds, but since Malcolmson and the copycats, the numbers had grown. Now Yvonne's car had to crawl past a crowd that seethed right up to the ribboned line watched by extra security guards.

"This isn't the help we need!"

"Stop coercing the elderly!"

"Rehabilitation, not lobotomies!"

Yvonne put her hands over her ears. She had nothing to do with client intake, consent, last wishes, but she knew the process was thorough. The lawyers had to provide every possible parachute, escape hatch, eject button, and knotted sheet, legally speaking, before the client's arborification was approved. But these shouting people acted as though she were murdering clients, when all she was trying to do was care for them. She knew just as well as the protestors that life might have been hard on arborification clients. That was *why* it mattered. Why couldn't they see that?

She knew she'd get in trouble, maybe even fired, if she shouted back, but it was hard to quiet her mind. *DON'T YOU KNOW THEY'RE PEOPLE*, she thought at top volume as she passed a chant of "Shut! It! Down!" *LET THEM REST.*

Bam bam bam. One of them had got close enough to rap a palm against her window. Yvonne shrank. Whoever it was got pulled back quickly, but had left a smear on the glass. Back home in her carport, Yvonne tried to rub the handprint with her sleeve, but that only made it worse. Exasperated, she glanced around to see if anyone had followed her, then hurried inside.

Yvonne heated up some noodles for herself and got drunk on coverage of the attacks, new and old, as she did every night. Trees hacked and splattered in the Malcolmson style. Trunks tagged in dripping neon. Scoring and scratch marks. In one case, a knife was buried in the tree, birch sap trailing from the wound. Someone had even tried to burn a grove and almost set the neighbourhood alight.

Because Malcolmson himself wasn't saying a word, the copycats interpreted his vandalism however they liked. "Arborification has been wrong from the start," a young man with eerily calm eyes pronounced into a microphone. "Just because we *can* do something doesn't mean we should."

Another clip, this time a woman scowling as the wind kept blowing hair into her face. "The science of arborification isn't our primary concern," she said. "What we question is the vetting process involved. Who gets sent to these facilities, and why? Is it truly consensual? Are they well treated? We keep getting the government runaround about privacy. What are they keeping secret?"

Yvonne stayed locked to the news as light faded from the world, only going to bed when her watch chirped a reminder that she had to wake up in four hours.

" 'Now, some final thoughts for each of you. Giselle, I want you to remember...' "

Ms. Moyo has sent the class a letter once a week throughout her medical leave. Every time, she ends with a few sentences for each person in the class, the same way she's given everyone their own special job in the classroom. Naima makes sure everyone's outdoor shoes are tidy, for example, and Ricardo is responsible for getting all the classroom books put back on the shelf.

Yvonne is in charge of the plants. This is her second job with the class. Her first was to make sure all the scissors were back in the bin at the end of the day. But one afternoon when Frankie O wouldn't give his pair back, Yvonne twisted it out of his hand, scraping a long red line down his thumb. Ms. Moyo shuffled that job to someone else, but asked Yvonne to stay late the next day and walked her through caring for the line of plants at the window. One lesson at a time: water, fertilizer, spraying for mites, how they like it when you talk to them. Now, whenever Yvonne feels upset in class, wants to shout at a classmate for misunderstanding her, or balls up homework sheets she's struggling with, she takes a breath and thinks about the plants, about every new leaf and bud that is quietly growing, about how they need her.

The substitute is droning on, the words mushing together for Yvonne as the letter goes through students one by one. She waits to hear her name. Surely she will be the next one... the next one... the next...

The next day after work, Yvonne changed into an oversized hoodie that she hoped would shield her face. She didn't think anyone would recognize her, but if there were protestors at the grove, she didn't want to take any chances.

The deputy minister had advised them to avoid visiting arborified sites, but hadn't made a specific rule against it. His words had the opposite of the intended effect on Yvonne: she felt ashamed that she hadn't been brave enough to visit any of her local groves since the protests had begun.

The whole way to the park, she raked her teeth over her bottom lip, squeezing the pinpoint of pain where she had broken the skin the day before. What would she do if there were other people there? Worse, what if it was too late, if the trees were already marked and abused? And if this grove was okay, what about all the others?

The grove she chose was hidden in a generous suburban park. Yvonne stared at her sneakers as she followed the cedar-chip path into the thin forest. Luckily for her, it was a snippy day for summer, with heavy cloud cover and a mean wind. Not many people out except lone dog walkers.

In her peripheral vision, the poplars lapsed into birch. Yvonne's head snapped up before she could think better of it— before she could decide for sure if she wanted to look or not and prepare herself for the worst—

—to see the grove quiet, gloriously intact.

The clean, long-lived trunks drew a relieved sigh from Yvonne.

Too late, she saw that there was another woman standing at the edge of the grove. She turned to smile at Yvonne.

"You were worried too," the woman said. She was about Yvonne's age, but better presented, with smooth hair and a fancy scarf.

Yvonne gulped and looked back to the trees as she nodded.

"The news has been awful," said the woman. "I don't think people understand…"

Yvonne shifted from foot to foot, the wind stinging her ears. She wanted to go up to each tree and greet them, but she knew that her behaviour would look odd to the other woman, so she held her place and touched each tree with her gaze instead. This was an old grove, planted before Yvonne had been hired, branches wide and venerable.

"My great-aunt's one of them," said the woman.

"Wait—one of these?" asked Yvonne. "How do you know?"

"Well, I don't, I guess," the other woman said, sounding a little embarrassed. "They don't release those records. They don't even track them, apparently. But I followed it as closely as I could, and it's the right age, at least."

Yvonne opened her mouth to tell the woman that it wasn't likely—that even back when this grove was planted, most plantings weren't in municipal parks but went to reforestation projects far from the public's eye—but the woman went on.

"She was a bit of a kook, you know, but she was very sure about this. Look, this is going to sound a little weird, but could you take a picture of me?" The woman held her phone out to Yvonne, even though they were still standing several steps apart.

"Why?" said Yvonne.

"There's this thing I saw online, people are tying ribbons around trees and taking pictures, to counteract the violence, you know?"

Yvonne didn't know, but she nodded anyway. Her screens only seemed to come up with pictures of groves that had been attacked, not whatever this woman was talking about. Her arm was still outstretched, hovering in the expanse between them. Reluctantly, Yvonne stepped forward to take the device.

The woman smiled her thanks and walked to the closest tree, laying her fingers against the white bark.

"But you don't know if that's her," said Yvonne. "Your aunt."

The woman pulled a blue ribbon out of her purse. Yvonne's throat caught. "Of course," said the woman. "But any one of these trees *might* be her, and that's good enough for me." She started winding the ribbon around one of the branches. Yvonne felt as though the loops were roping her own forearm.

"There," said the woman, tying a careful bow before turning to Yvonne with a camera-ready smile.

Gingerly, Yvonne lifted the phone to head height, the screen blurring as it tried to focus. The woman stood beside the tree, the blue ribbon companionably at shoulder height. As Yvonne's thumb hovered over the snap button, a wind gusted, freezing her ungloved hands and flattening the ribbon loops into whipping lines. The woman kept her smile in place but squinted, lifting a hand to tidy her hair.

"No, no, you can't!" exclaimed Yvonne, rushing to the tree's side and shoving the phone into the woman's chest. Yvonne began picking apart the bow with stiff, panicked fingers. "I know you mean well, but—you can't tie up a tree just for a picture—it'll choke." She unwound the ribbon from the branch. "And this feels synthetic, too, so if it fell off it wouldn't biodegrade, or it could affect other wildlife, didn't you think of that?"

The woman stepped back as Yvonne scrunched the ribbon and wheeled towards her. "Okay," the woman said, her hands in front of her, palms down. "Okay, yes, I hear you, I hadn't considered that."

But Yvonne, expecting more resistance, carried onwards. "And for a picture? Just a picture? You don't even know where your aunt is, and it doesn't matter anyway, they're all at peace now, don't you see that it's the whole grove that we need to love, that a ribbon won't protect anything?"

She took a breath as a new realization hit her. "Actually, most people probably don't even know that this is an arborified grove, your ribbon would tell them, and then they'd know, *then they'd know* and they might attack this one too, we just have to let them be, they've escaped everything that could hurt them, just leave them alone…"

Yvonne's head hurt. Some hair had escaped her ponytail and flapped across her face; she clawed it behind her ears, unsuccessfully.

"Okay, you're right," the woman said. "Let's just leave the trees as they are."

Yvonne nodded and sniffed. She yanked the drawstrings on her hoodie to hug the cloth around her face.

"I'm going to go now," said the woman in a delicate tone, although she didn't move. "Did you know anyone arborified here? Or—wherever."

Yvonne swallowed. A stiff nod. Yes. Someone. Yes. All of them. Yes.

The woman said a soft goodbye and walked away at last, her question a thorn in Yvonne's mind.

Then she realized that she had been twisting the ribbon between her hands this whole time. The woman was out of sight already. Not wanting to throw the ribbon out, Yvonne carried it home, stuffing it at the back of a junk drawer so that she'd never have to see it again.

" 'To Yvonne,' " the substitute teacher reads out at last. Yvonne's breath catches and her face blooms hot. " 'You have a great deal of kindness inside of you. Remember that when you feel angry. Take care of the plants.' "

After the encounter with the woman at the grove, Yvonne looked up the ribbon campaign, and it upset her almost as much as the vandals did. Everyone was missing the point.

She started polite, advising people against tying foreign objects to trees. But when people called her names, her responses got angrier, telling them they were empty do-gooders who were only fuelling the Shut It Down movement. Only at 3:00 a.m., when a network of lonely neighbourhood dogs started to chorus, was she able to blink the screen's glare from her eyes and step away.

Two days later, her director called her into his office. He was about ten years older than her, a man with a comfortably worn demeanour. Not a bad guy, Yvonne had always thought, but the grim line of his mouth set her heart racing.

He had printouts for her, spread on the desk between them. All of her after-hours comments. More of them were in all caps than she remembered.

"Yvonne," he said, gently, after letting a silence pool between them. "Are you okay?"

"It's just…" Yvonne gestured helplessly. "They don't understand!"

"I know," he said. "But you know our media policy. My boss told me that I should suspend you for this."

"No! You can't—"

He held a hand up. "I told her I wouldn't, that she'd have to fire me first. We need you, Yvonne, but I have to know that you're okay to do your job, and that you'll delete all of this." He tapped the pile.

"But if they… I have to do something, they're talking about cancelling the whole program. Closing the..." She couldn't finish.

"The most important thing you can do is what you were doing before. I don't disagree with you, you know that. But getting angry doesn't help anything. We already have people arguing our side, through the right channels."

He sighed and leaned back. "The truth is, these things are bigger than us, Yvonne," he said. "It's noisy right now, but this will die down. Comms says that it's already waning. We just notice because we care."

"But everyone should care."

"Sure. These people do, even if they think differently than you."

"That's not the same."

Exasperation crossed the director's face. Oh no: she was going to lose him too. His tone soured a little. "Yvonne, I'm not going to suspend you, but this has to stop, okay? Forget about these people. You're here for the clients, right? Focus on that."

Yvonne looked down from his annoyance, her hands cold. Yes, of course, he was right. The trees. She was here for the trees, and she hoped to be there for them for the rest of her life.

" 'I'm sorry that I wasn't able to finish the school year with you, my friends, or see you grow into future grades and beyond. I hope you will visit me sometime.' " The substitute teacher frowns, but her brow clears as she continues reading. " 'Now, it's true that I won't be planted in public for a few years, and even then, you won't know which tree is me. So I have a favour to ask from all of you. This is how we can stay in touch. Whenever you see a birch tree, say hello. Touch the trunk if you're able. You never know. Someday it might be me. And if it isn't, a friendly hello is a precious gift to share.' "

By the time Malcolmson was sentenced almost two years later, the public had lost interest. Yvonne enjoyed the news privately, having learned not to expect much from her colleagues. At the facility, job anxiety had smoothed back into complacency as the Shut It Down tagline went stale, a slogan chained to a receding year.

The judge gave Malcolmson a hefty fine, four hundred hours of community service, six months of prison, and a thorough upbraiding. *What you've done is inexcusable and unforgiveable,* she had said. *It's as though you defiled a grave, or burned a canary alive in its cage. I hope you examine your actions and decide how to be a better human being.*

Yvonne cheered the condemnation, although it wasn't how she would have put it. The trees weren't a grave, or a cage. If anything, they were more like... angel wings, unfurling in a thousand fresh leaves every spring. It was freedom, not bondage; life, not death.

It was too late for the trees Malcolmson had killed and scarred, and for the many other trees injured in the surge of anger that followed his attack. Still, the harsh sentence would serve as a template for the other vandals, all waiting their turn.

That day Yvonne told the trees, with conviction at last, that justice was served. They were safe. And she could continue to care for them for the next ten, twenty...

...thirty years. When she had time, Yvonne still liked to witness the new arrivals. She'd begun to think about which season would be her last—and she knew the staff wondered too. She resisted making retirement plans, but she was slowing down, and even part-time work was getting harder with her arthritic hands and knees.

Yvonne took her breaks in the small patio enclosed by benches and planters, deadheading the annuals with only her fingers and thumbs as snippers. It made her look busy when the client vans pulled up.

The white vans hadn't changed much over the years—just that there were more of them—and neither had the security guards, an endless replication of fresh-faced youths. She knew they weren't the *same* young people, of course, just like the intake team had changed over many times in her career.

There—Yvonne ducked behind a geranium—the clients, shuffling off the van. Her future charges. Grey heads. Some younger people, but not healthy ones. Thin, muted, haunted. Soon soothed by soil and sunlight.

Yvonne frowned. Something about the group snagged her thoughts as she scanned the individuals from her oblique vantage point. Nothing out of the ordinary, really—one tall man, youngish, in his fifties, maybe, a skinny neck craning forward, exposing the long smudge of his hairline...

She gulped, her fist twisting a flower stalk, as she remembered the broken trees, the blood-spattered stumps.

Rawling. Rawling Malcolmson.

She hadn't thought of that time in years, her mind always skipping away whenever the memories floated back. Demonstrations against arborification were unheard of these days.

What was he *doing* here?

She stared at his aged appearance before he disappeared into the reception centre. A few days of procedures, medical and legal, and he would be on her field, in her hands.

The rest of the day, Malcolmson was all Yvonne could think about. How could she face him, even in his arborified state? All the hurt and betrayal from his actions years ago stewed inside her, interfering with her need to do her job properly, tend the untended, care for the unwanted.

She was shocked that no one else had recognized him—the clerks and lawyers had access to his full name, even—but when she stopped to consider it, she couldn't think of anyone who had been working here in the Shut It Down era. It had been more than thirty years. Most of her colleagues had been children, or not even born, the last time the facility had been threatened.

As soon as she got home, without even bothering to change, she huddled on the couch and scraped up all the old coverage she could find. The bloody trunks, the vandalism and graffiti, the protests, counter-protests, Shut It Down flyers, the ribbon campaign. The long editorials and then, abruptly, the slide back into irrelevance. She was surprised at how small it seemed now, a brief media sizzle that had quickly gone flat.

Searches for Malcolmson himself had paltry results. A mention in his mother's obituary. An out-of-date contact for what might have been a pyramid scheme. A listing in the back of a long-dead community plan. When her increasingly esoteric searches came up with nothing one time too many, she smashed her fist against the screen. As it rainbowed from the impact, she pulled her hand to her chest, her eyes itching with tears.

The day of the planting, Yvonne woke up knowing that she would have to face Malcolmson. His mind would be calmed. He would be clad in undyed linen, pliant, barefoot, awaiting the peace and care of arborification.

She called in sick.

No one gave her a hard time, and she knew that her chief was more than capable of overseeing the work. They didn't realize how monumental this was. Yvonne had never missed a planting, not once in almost fifty years.

Of course, there was nothing physically wrong with her. But thinking of his features felt like a cold slime under her skin: his dejected form, the way he had slouched into the reception centre, the bunched architecture of his face. That same sinister hairline.

Avoiding work was as bad as going. She never knew what to do with herself when she had a day of forced inactivity. Spurting restlessly between watching TV and housework, Yvonne couldn't tear her mind away from Malcolmson, what he had started, how he had threatened the very existence of arborification. And now he was back, wanting it for himself!

Scrubbing her kitchen sink: how could she tend him—*him*—the way she did every other person who came into her care?

Scrolling irritably through sitcoms: but was his case different from anyone else she had helped in her long career?

Descaling her showerhead: no doubt she had assisted others who were guilty of worse crimes, or who were blighted with thoughtless sins—cruelty, greed, self-absorption.

Peeling carrots: now the thought of him would contaminate his entire cohort.

The next day, Yvonne rode into work past the familiar lines of birch, their clean perfection hurtful. The newest trees were like any other freshly planted grove she had tended. From their constellation of origins, they had all converged here: forty-odd souls who had agreed to the simple release of life as a tree.

Yvonne glimpsed him immediately as she walked up to the new grove. That long, close-cropped head. She looked away. Her chief was reporting on the planting—minor concerns here and there, nothing to be alarmed about, a good healthy group all around—and Yvonne did her best to pay attention. She was creating a bubble around Malcolmson, erasing him. She would not see him, or touch him, or connect with him the way she did with every other tree. Her secret vengeance. It would have to be enough.

"Whoa, Yvonne, are you okay?"

Yvonne regained her balance after stumbling into her colleague. It was what's-her-name, the new girl, newish, new two years ago. Her eyes flickered with concern, her hands wide as though to catch Yvonne.

"I'm fine," said Yvonne. She pulled her hat on more snugly and glared. "Just the heat, I think."

"Do you need a break? I can get you some water—"

"I said I'm fine!" Yvonne turned away to walk along the grove she had been inspecting. It hadn't been the heat, although springs seemed hotter than ever these days. She had been avoiding looking at Malcolmson and hadn't seen where she was stepping.

She thought she'd been bricking up her hatred, but the more he changed, the more irritable she felt. He'd progressed smoothly over the last ten weeks, and soon he would be indistinguishable from the others. Even though she knew where he was planted here at the facility, one day he would be mingled with other trees and shipped out, his identity lost for good.

Yvonne paced down the line of trees, a few steps beyond Malcolmson, then swinging back to pass him again. Leaf-shadow speckled her feet.

How dare he think he deserved arborification, after what he had done?

Her pockets jostled as she turned and paced back again, catching against her leg. She reached in to rearrange the items —keys, clippers, communicator.

She stopped in front of his tree, looking at it properly for the first time. Wormtrails of sweat tickled her neck.

A good, healthy tree, no different from the others.

She pulled out her clippers, squeezing and releasing to open their half-moon blade.

Disgust rose in her throat. She couldn't go another day, not another hour, even, without—without—*something.*

For a moment, she thought of stabbing the tree, tearing at the new wood, making him as ugly as she knew him to be.

But no. That was excessive. She didn't need to be violent.

Before thinking any further, Yvonne knelt. She might have been tying her shoe. Holding the clippers at their crosspiece, she touched the point to the tree's fresh bark, only a few inches from the ground.

Baby flesh. She paused to let the thought drift away. Then, ready again, she pressed the blade a little harder into the tree, feeling a soft pop as it punctured the outer layer. Somewhere inside her, groundwater level, she knew she was making a mistake. Too late: she was slicing a vertical line. It was unnervingly easy, the newly grown skin parting smoothly under the blade.

Her first thought had been to carve an M into the tree, an ugly zigzag to suit the degenerate Malcolmson. But after scoring the first line, the memory of her grade three teacher, dear Ms. Moyo, floated back, her beautiful looping handwriting, the sunny afternoons Yvonne had spent caring for the class plants. Swallowing, Yvonne changed course: an M wouldn't do. Instead, she added two branching lines to turn the mark into an even-armed Y, her own secret symbol.

"Yvonne?"

She jolted at the interruption, dropping the clippers into the dirt, *paff.* "What?"

It was the new girl again. What was her name—Emily? "Sorry. Margot's looking for you. In the east field."

"Fine," said Yvonne, grabbing the clippers, then standing and brushing dirt off her pants. She tried to position her legs so that they blocked the carved mark from Emily's view. "Anything else?"

"Uh—no," said Emily, but she didn't move. Her gaze wandered past Yvonne to the trees behind her. Yvonne's breath froze in fear.

"Yes?"

"It's such a beautiful thing, isn't it?" said Emily. She took a step toward one of the trees—not Malcolmson, thank god— and placed her palm on the trunk. "You get used to it, working here every day, but it hits you sometimes... such a beautiful, beautiful thing..."

"Don't you have a job to do?"

It came out more rudely than Yvonne intended. As Emily stammered a reply,

Yvonne backpedalled with a hasty, "Thank you, Emily."

Emily was already walking away, but she paused to say over her shoulder, "It's Emma."

Yvonne waited until Emma/Emily was a safe distance away before she turned to check Malcolmson, scuffing away the depressions her knees had left in the dirt. The Y mark was weeping sap, but from standing, it was barely noticeable. It would do.

As she left, her hand automatically reached out towards the trunk—but she pulled back before she made contact.

It was a small thing, that mark: three scored lines, less than an inch across. In all the wide, deep, rich world, just three little lines!

But when Yvonne closed her eyes, it was all she could see. Those lines were giant to her. They had obliterated Malcolmson's whippet neck, his damp eyes, his cruel mouth. Now he was three sap-filled scratches, gashing every thought she had.

Yvonne became more distracted at work. She directed the wrong field to be fertilized on Tuesday, forgot a meeting on Thursday. Arrived late on Friday because she had left her pass at home. Distantly, she knew they were building the case for her senility, and how could she tell management the true cause of her sloppiness?

When she closed her eyes at night, memories pressed into her darkness. The carnage of Malcolmson's attacks, the Shut It Down hysteria. Her past director confronting her with piles of her online shouting. A long red mark on Frankie O's hand. And a sliced Y, one that was scarring her as much as it did Malcolmson. More, perhaps.

Shame tunnelled deeper into Yvonne. The years hadn't healed her—they had only fooled her.

She knew what she had to do.

By the time Yvonne was sitting down with one of their in-house lawyers, Benni, the envelope containing her last wishes was already thumbed with worry. It had taken her three tries to set it down correctly.

She had requested this lawyer specifically because Benni had a reputation for empathy, more interested in the spirit than the letter of the law. Yvonne was surprised to find how generously staff accommodated her arborification request, allowing procedural exceptions to help smooth the process. She didn't have to arrive in a van, of course, and she could complete the paperwork at any time, although she would still receive the injections on the same day as the rest of her group.

Benni went through the paperwork as she would for any other client. All the rights that Yvonne would relinquish. What would happen to the possessions she left behind. Next of kin: none.

Yvonne barely listened as the lawyer described every nub and nodule of the law, waiting for the moment when Benni paused, her eyes warm, and asked if Yvonne had any questions.

Yvonne lifted the envelope from her lap to the table.

"Just one special request," she whispered.

No one spoke in the waiting room. Yvonne had never been to this part of the facility before. It was restricted, and she never had any reason to come. This wasn't the main reception space—she had skipped that phase—but the smaller waiting room, the one before clients were called away to the private session with the doctor.

The man beside her cleared his throat. The oxygen tank on the woman in the corner hissed and sighed, a soothing sound in the sterile space, almost like the pulse of ocean waves.

Yvonne was one of them now. Wherever they came from, her fellow clients, they were here now, haphazardly together. A someday grove. Yvonne's fingers floated up a little from her knee. Absurd here, of course, but she felt her familiar refrain. *Hello. Hello, my friend. Hello...*

"Yvonne?"

Her turn. Yvonne stood, followed the nurse, and disappeared.

Benni took last requests seriously. The tree in question—the tree that had once been Yvonne—was in the far corner of the grove. Benni had visited her several times earlier in the transformation. Week by week, Yvonne's face had smoothed into the fresh skin of birchbark; her frame winnowed to a slender pole; branches and leaves sprouted skyward.

No time to dawdle today. Benni found the tree, dropped to one knee, and pulled out a paring knife. She touched the blank spot where she would leave the symbol that Yvonne had requested. Benni ran a finger through the dew pearling the soft bark, tracking the even-armed Y, remembering Yvonne's old brown hands, her skittery gaze, her clumsy, earnest voice.

The air was fresh here in the groves. Benni took a deep breath, then started to carve.

See Cadence Mandybura's story "Arborify"
online at Metaphorosis.
If you liked it, leave a comment. Authors love
that!
Remember to subscribe to our e-mail updates so
you'll know when new stories are posted.

About the story

This story began about five years ago with a few paragraphs describing a woman tending to planted people. I was fascinated by the core concept of a government program that lets people choose to become trees (perhaps because I was working in government at the time), but was frankly intimidated at how to turn the idea into a meaningful story. I'm a worldbuilder to a fault, so spent much of my writing time thinking through the ramifications and moral greyness of such a program—is it compassionate or wildly dystopic? How would citizens respond to such a program? Would good intentions fray into corruption over time?

Ultimately, I wanted to leave many of these questions for the reader to contemplate rather than have the story provide definitive answers. "Arborify" ended up being a much more personal story about Yvonne's relationship with the trees, exploring themes of care and neglect, innocence and guilt, and what connects us as individuals and as a society.

A question for the author

Q: Do you use music for inspiration? If so, what do you listen to?

A: Absolutely, music is a key part of my process when I'm generating new writing. (For revising, I need quiet.) My go-to writing playlist consists of oud music by artists like Anouar Brahem, Le Trio Joubran, Faran Ensemble, and Naseer Shamma. I usually start with

Brahem's "Conte de l'Incroyable Amour," a gorgeous ten-minute piece that helps me settle into my writing. I also love Western classical music for writing (Bach, Dvořák, and Rachmaninov are perennial favourites), and if I'm trying to tap into a particular mood, I turn to ambient sounds, such as swamp noises or a looped version of the Sardaukar chant from *Dune*.

About the author

Cadence Mandybura writes speculative fiction with a fondness for both beauty and absurdity. She works as an editor and is the associate producer of the fiction anthology podcast *The Truth*. To unwind, she enjoys drumming, including taiko and a range of Latin and West African instruments.

www.cadencemandybura.com, @cade_bura

Astrid Underwater

J.J. Eskelin

The day Sigun lost her son in the water, it was unusually warm, even for August. She had driven with him up the Olympic Peninsula to a park just over the bridge, on the western shore of Kilisut Island. The little island had been created some fifty years before, when a ship canal was dredged through a backwater marsh, severing the land from the Olympic Peninsula.

Now, a sand bar, bleached and desolate, edged the deep canal. The sand bar was littered with empty shells and strewn with bone-white driftwood tumbled smooth by water. In between the sand bar and the rocky shore of the little island, tidal rivers wove through the sand and rock. Beneath their sparkling waters every surface was generously carpeted with life; the rocks were sharp with oysters, dressed with purple sea anemones, slippery with green and brown algae.

Sigun, tall and strong, carried Erik easily as she waded through the seawater streams, stepping gingerly over the life-encrusted rocks, out towards the sand bar. Once there, Erik set about busily reorganizing the driftwood into a fort. A constant monologue accompanied his work, demanding no response. She was lucky in this, that he could play alone.

Erik had been terrified of the water all summer. Sigun had not been able to get him to even dip his beautiful pink toes into the sea. Swimming lessons had been a complete disaster. Erik had taken a particular dislike to the last swim instructor who had attempted to force him into the pool. Before Sigun could intervene, Erik had started screaming. "I hate her! I hate her! I hate her!" His cry had echoed like a curse in the vaulted chamber above the indoor pool.

Sigun had been ready to concede defeat when the director of the Aquatic Center himself had emerged from the water. While the swim instructors had been barely out of childhood, the director was a man with closely cut hair and a stiff beard of shining silver. He was short, smaller than Sigun, but his presence was commanding. He was perfectly formed, every muscle outlined by his black shorty wetsuit. The skin of his exposed arms and legs was smooth bronze, his face ageless. A trident would not have looked out of place in his hand, Sigun had thought, amused at the image.

"Come, Erik," the director, Mr. Merehinen, had ordered in a low, even voice. He was devoid of the false cheer and friendliness that often seem a prerequisite for working with small children. Yet Erik had not hesitated; he had taken the man's cold hand and stepped willingly into the water at last.

Sigun had never been afraid of the water. She was an excellent swimmer, and an even better sailor, having grown up sailing her father's boats. She loved the water, but she understood the danger of it, the vigilance and respect it commanded. So, even if she had good reason to believe Erik would not touch the water, she did not intend to close her eyes while he played so close to the lapping waves of the deep canal.

As she watched Erik, her back rested against a driftwood log, warm from the sunshine. Sigun slipped her feet out of her sandals and anchored them in the coarse sand. Erik had been awake in the night again and Sigun was deeply tired. Keeping her eyes open against the onslaught of the sun and sparkling water was unbearably painful.

Suddenly, Sigun was jolted awake. A cloud had eclipsed the sun, the rocks were gray and cold, and the trees above the shoreline were dark emerald, almost black. She was shivering.

"Erik?" she called out, leaping up. "Erik!" she screamed, running around the piles of pale dead wood, raking the black water with her eyes, her stomach accelerating through the bottom of her feet.

"Erik!" There was no answer. Even in the summer, the Salish Sea is deadly cold. It takes only a few seconds for a child to drown. Shame and guilt broke into a torrent beneath her terror. The loss of another child would be unpardonable. Unbearable. She wanted to tear her heart out from her body.

Too much time had passed, but Sigun ruthlessly repressed her panic. If she was to have any chance of saving him, she had to keep her head. She bounded out into the water, the sharp shells cutting her feet, until she felt the seabed drop into the deep, icy canal. The surface of the sea was unforgivably still. The world was colorless. The trees were black against the grey sky.

Then Sigun heard splashing behind her, and Erik's laughter. She turned and scooped him up into her arms, every dear, precious, inch of him soaking wet. Sigun crushed his cold, damp body against her racing heart. She was filled with a mixture of relief, joy, and rage so overwhelming she was speechless. She felt sick.

"Erik, where were you?" she whispered hoarsely, holding him tightly against her breast as she carried him back to the barren sand bar, over the slippery stones and the rocks sheltering spiney assemblies of black-purple sea urchins, until he struggled to wiggle free of her arms. She was shaking as she set him down on the bone-dry rocks beside her backpack. "You know not to go into the water alone!"

"I wasn't alone," he answered unconcerned, but his lips were blue. She dug into the backpack, pulling out the extra set of clothing she always carried for him. She helped him dress and handed him a tart green apple, which he happily accepted. He bit into the crisp fruit, the juice running down his sea-damp chin.

"If you can't see me, I can't see you." Sigun didn't want to make him afraid again, and she was careful not to sound as terrified and angry as she felt. "It is good to be in the water, but you *must* have someone in with you." Sigun was strapping her bleeding feet back into her sandals and packing up their things. She lifted Erik up, and tucking him under her arm, forded the tidal rivers back to the shore. Their car was parked, dusty and alone, on the gravel underneath the long arms of a giant Madrona tree, whose red bark had peeled back to reveal smooth wood that glistened like tanned, wet skin.

Sigun settled Erik into his car seat, fastening the harness. "I wasn't alone." He handed Sigun the core of the apple. "She was with me."

"Who was with you, Erik?" Sigun asked as she fastened her seatbelt, glancing up at his reflection in the rear view mirror.

"The mermaid," he said. Sigun pulled away from the park, and drove quickly up the gravel road and over the bridge. She was still fighting the afterburn of terror, and in its place shame and anger were settling into her body. She, Lars Havegrimm's daughter, had almost lost her child in the water. It was unforgivable.

"Did the mermaid have a tail?" Sigun's heart rate was returning to normal. Maybe Erik had seen a harbor seal, or some other creature swimming below the water, and had been curious, as Sigun would have been. Sigun was a marine biologist after all, or at least, she had been one.

"No," Erik laughed as if her question had been ridiculous.

"Well, what did it look like, then?"

Erik was kicking his legs into the seat in front of him. "Like you," he said, "Her eyes were green, but brighter. Her hair was long, but darker. Her teeth were whiter—" He had his hand in his mouth, feeling his own teeth. "—and sharper."

She glanced at him quickly in the rearview mirror to see if he was as disturbed as she was by his imagined encounter, and was struck as she was every now and then by how impossibly dear he was to her. He looked healthy and unconcerned, as if he had not just been pulled, blue-lipped, out of the cold sea.

"You know her, Mama. It was Astrid," Erik said, his angelic brow furrowed in frustration, his foot kicking the back of the seat with renewed vigor. "She found me."

"Astrid?" Sigun jerked the car back into her lane just in time. A truck sailed past on her left, its honking horn distorted by the speed of their near collision. It took all of Sigun's concentration, then, to drive safely home.

Astrid, Erik's twin sister. Astrid who had lived only eight days. Astrid who had been sedated, wrapped in tubes, and placed in a glass box, floors above Sigun's ravaged body. Astrid who had drowned, not in the water, but in the air.

Unlike Erik, who had been born looking like a shriveled elf, skinny and jaundiced, a tiny wizened old man with pointy ears and a piercing scream, Astrid had been born beautiful and healthy looking. But she had been born second, pulled, violently, feet first, out of Sigun, unwilling and unready. Her lungs had never made the transition from the liquid world of Sigun's womb.

The sky was darkening and little drops of rain began to hit the windshield as she drove over the bridge onto the large island where they lived. She wound her way carefully down to the southern tip of it, the roads dark and narrow, lined with towering trees. It had begun to rain in earnest, and it was hours before Tom would be home from the city.

When Tom did come home, he was soaking wet, having biked back from the ferry in the worst of the downpour. He was exhausted, but the shadows under his eyes did not diminish his good looks. If anything, Tom was growing more handsome. Sigun almost resented it, that his beauty was increasing as she felt hers to be fading. Her hand moved involuntarily to the silver streak that ran through her dark red hair. It had seemed to appear suddenly, the day she finally came home from the hospital without Astrid. Motherhood had changed the geography of her body inside and out like an earthquake, a volcanic eruption. The cost of it had fallen on her physically, heavily. Sigun, enveloped in grief, had experienced so little of the joy of it.

She had once been sure of Tom's desire, but now she was no longer confident it was under her sway at all. Although the truth was, for some time she had not cared. Sigun felt much less like a siren than a fury.

It was only at the beginning of the summer that she had finally weaned Erik. She had been warned she might suffer a sort of withdrawal; her body had been a factory of calming hormones. Perhaps that was why she felt a storm building inside her, a tumult swirling in her blood. Perhaps that was why Astrid's apparition felt so unsettling, a sudden burst of turbulence when she was already in the middle of a storm.

Later that night, as Sigun and Tom lay in bed together, he asked her about her day.

"It was fine. We drove to Kilisut Island."

"Did you see anything interesting?"

"Well... Erik thought he saw a mermaid."

Tom laughed. "I shouldn't have taken him to the Olde Curiosity Shop."

The shop was on the wharf near where the ferry left the city for the big island where they lived. Among its curiosities had been a 'mermaid', a taxidermist's chimera of fish and monkey, its sharp little teeth bared in fury at the customers below. It had seemed obscene, even in Sigun's childhood.

Sigun rolled onto her back, hesitating. "But the strangest thing was... Erik called the mermaid Astrid."

Tom stilled beside her. "Astrid? Do you and Erik talk about Astrid?"

"No, never. Do you?"

"Of course not. But Erik is like a little sponge. He must have heard us mention her name." She turned away from him, onto her side, and he curled around her. She couldn't bring herself to share how close she had come to losing Erik, the terror and shame of it. Not yet. Sigun could feel his body settle as he fell quickly into a deep sleep, the privilege of the exhausted and the innocent. Eventually, and with great effort, she followed him into oblivion.

The next morning Sigun set about with renewed determination to get Erik swimming lessons with the director of the Aquatic Center. If nothing else, she could make sure Erik learned to swim.

"He doesn't give lessons anymore," the scheduler at the Aquatic Center said, sounding bored. Despite Mr. Merehinen's flat affect and lack of good cheer, which some parents found disturbing, he had a reputation on the island for being able to teach the children to swim in a fraction of the time of other instructors. After one of his students had gone on to compete in the Olympics, the clamor of families wanting to work with him had become an annoyance, and he had stopped teaching altogether.

"Would you please ask him to consider it?" Astrid persisted. "He is the only person who has been able to lure Erik into the water."

To the obvious surprise of the Aquatic Centre's scheduler, her request was granted, and on the following Tuesday, Sigun and Erik set out for his first lesson.

As they stood at the rim of the pool waiting, Erik held her hand, leaning hesitantly towards the water.

"Are you ready, Erik?" said a gruff voice from the pool. Sigun turned and met the gaze of the director standing in the water. His hair was glowing metallic in the light that filtered down from the skylights in the high cathedral ceiling. His eyes glinted like pale green sea glass in his copper face.

"Good morning, Mr. Merehinen." Sigun was careful to politely keep her eyes on his face, above the collar of his skin-tight neoprene suit. He nodded tersely and held out his hand past her, unsmiling, to Erik.

"Come, Erik," Mr. Merehinen said. Once again, the small boy took the man's hand and jumped into the water.

When Mr. Merehinen brought Erik back to the steps of the pool at the end of the lesson, he cast an assessing glance up at Sigun. He stepped out of the pool after Erik, water dripping off his body.

"We can continue lessons for now." Mr. Merehinen didn't seem pleased or displeased. Sigun felt relieved, as if they had passed some sort of test.

"Thank you. This is important to us." Sigun blushed. She sounded overly earnest even to herself.

But Mr. Merehinen had already turned away and quickly disappeared, past the showers and the nurse's station, into the bowels of the swimming hall.

The next morning, Sigun and Erik took the ferry across to the city to visit her father, Lars, and her grandmother Tulikki, her mother's mother, who had helped raise her. The plan was for Sigun to accompany her grandmother to a long-anticipated art exhibition while her father and Erik walked to the Ballard Locks to ogle ships and boats passing up and down between Lake Washington and the Salish Sea.

Sigun drove first to Tulikki's little yellow house, northeast of Green Lake. A giant birch tree dominated her front yard, towering over the house. This was Tulikki's Yard Tree, and following the old customs, she gave it offerings: coffee, milk, vodka, and occasionally, Sigun suspected, blood.

Most people had forgotten such traditions, but not Tulikki, who had been raised by her own grandmother. After Tulikki was orphaned by the Winter War, she and her grandmother had been sent from Finland to live with cousins north of Seattle. They had shared a little bed in a closet, more indentured servants than family, until Tulikki had saved enough money for their escape.

Even in Sigun's childhood, the Yard Tree had been a massive, flourishing thing, a testament to Tulikki's archaic superstitions. Sigun had said as much to her father one day as he had collected her from her grandmother's house. She had been looking back at the tree, so tall she could not see the top of it from the pickup's window.

"It's not your grandmother's witchcraft that makes that tree grow," her father had growled at Sigun, irritated. "It's her damned sewer line." Her father's angry dismissal had surprised her. Over time, Sigun had learned to be careful not to share Tulikki's little eccentricities with him. Sigun glanced up now at the tree as she walked beneath the green canopy and up the uneven stone steps to her grandmother's red door.

Tulikki popped, grinning, from the front door before Sigun's knuckles reached the red-painted wood. As Sigun helped her grandmother settle into the car with her packages, a magnificent smell of cardamom and butter emerged from her parcels. She had brought a basket of pastries, of course. She never visited Sigun's father without them. They were her special tithing, a penance for her daughter's desertion of Lars when Sigun was just a baby.

Lars was waiting outside when they pulled up to Havegrimm's shipyard. The shipyard had been founded a hundred years before by Lars's grandfather, Torsten Havegrimm, a master shipwright, and his younger brother who had come over from Norway together. The original sign for Havegrimm's Shipyard still dominated the front face of the office, carefully maintained and restored, like the old wooden boats within. On the sign, a wizened seal balanced a sailboat on its right-front flipper. Erik, as was his habit, greeted the seal happily, and it grinned back at him with a knowing twinkle in its eye.

The habitual glower of her father's weathered face broke into a smile as he took Erik's tiny hand. Lars was just over six and half feet tall and he loomed over little Erik and tiny Tulikki like a giant. His tousled, white-blond hair was a tangle beneath his old fisherman's cap, and his clothes and boots were dusty from work. After exchanging greetings, Lars and Erik set off eagerly for the locks, and Sigun and Tulikki turned east toward the museum.

The museum was newly built, a monument to the ideals of rational, Scandinavian modernity. As they entered the white curving walls, Tulikki said, "Do you remember when I read that children's version of the Kalevala to you?" The exhibition was of a Finnish painter, Akseli Gallen-Kallela, who was famous for his depictions of scenes from the epic poem. The Kalevala was the national epic of Finland, and it had been composed from bits of songs and spells collected throughout Finland some two hundred years before. Sigun vaguely remembered the strange tales: wizards battling through song, women forged from metal, jaw bones turned into harps.

"Of course," Sigun assured her, but Tulikki was already moving briskly between the paintings, pointing out this and cooing over that. Sigun trailed in her wake, happy to follow her irregular course as Tulikki paused to examine each work. Sigun liked best Gallen-Kallela's later paintings, finished after the death of his daughter, with their bold black lines and anguished figures. Her favorite was his depiction of the witch-woman Louhi, as a monster with the body and wings of an eagle, vicious talons, and braided red hair, hovering above a long ship sharp with spears.

They had seen almost everything, and Tulikki had finally begun to slow her pace, when she sailed right past the large triptych, three canvases enclosed in a massive, intricately carved and gilded frame. Sigun, curious, stopped to take a closer look. The object of the paintings was a young woman, pale and passive, naked in the last two panes. In the central painting, she was half in the water, twisting away from a man with a long white beard who was reaching out from a wooden fishing dory with grasping hands.

A bony hand gripped Sigun's arm, startling her.

"Do you know this story?" Tulikki said, not looking at Sigun, but at the painting with narrowed eyes. "It's the story of Aino, from the Kalevala. Her brother bargains her away to Väinämöinen, the old wizard, and her mother happily agrees to give her away in exchange for her son's life. Aino escapes by drowning herself and turning into a fish."

Where was the anger on Aino's face? Sigun felt it for her. The girl in the painting was a hairless creature, pale and innocent and as inured to loss as a wooden madonna in a medieval church.

"The model in this version is the painter Akseli Gallen-Kallela's own wife. A little bloodless, don't you think?" Tulikki cackled as she patted Sigun's arm. "It makes you wonder, doesn't it?"

"Shall we go outside to wait for the boys?" Sigun needed fresh air; she was already moving toward the door.

"Of course," Tulikki assented and took Sigun's arm, patting it again. Sigun had at least a dozen inches of height on her grandmother, and she checked her stride carefully to match Tulikki's as they moved down the ramp into the soaring entrance of the museum.

As they reached the towering entrance hall, the darkened glass doors parted to reveal her father, a dusty giant, out of place amidst the sparkling glass and high white walls of the modern museum. He held Erik in the crook of his arm, a beaming cherub riding on a thundercloud.

"Just on time!" Lars boomed, pleased as always by punctuality, his fearsome face breaking into a smile of large white teeth.

Their little procession stopped at the shipyard's messy office. Tulikki conjured her cardamom rolls from beneath a linen tea towel. A silent contentment fell over them, amidst the bliss of butter, sugar, cardamom, and coffee, until Erik, with crumbs on his face, demanded they get to work on the boats.

It was the end of the summer, and the shipyard was starting to fill up again. Boats were straggling back in from spending their summers in the archipelago, or from traveling up north to the raucous shores of the Canadian coast, where they had wandered past waterfalls crashing into the sea, orcas breaching the surface of hidden bays, waves lapping fondly on their wooden hulls. Havegrimm's dealt only with the upkeep and restoration of wooden boats. These boats, costly and difficult to maintain, were the obsessions of their owners; they sounded different in the water, more magical, more alive. Now they were home to be coddled over the winter at great expense.

Her father was working on a boat that had not been on the water that summer, nor for several years, by the look of it.

"Has this boat just been purchased?" Sigun asked, running her hand over the wood with its flaking paint.

"Nope. It's been with the same family since the beginning. But now someone finally has the money to restore it." Her father sounded pleased. He was carefully scraping off the peeling paint. "It will take some work to make it seaworthy again." He turned to Sigun, a sly look on his face. "Do you know who built this boat?"

She did. Even without recognizing the lines of the elegant little sloop, she would have known by the sparkle in her father's eye. "Grandpa Torsten," Sigun smiled back at her father.

"Otherwise I wouldn't have taken it on. But I know I can get this one back out on the water." He patted the wood fondly. "When's the last time you were out on a boat?" Lars did not look at Sigun, his gaze still fastened on his work.

"Oh, I don't know. It's hard to find the time." After college, Sigun had chosen to work on a humble research vessel rather than continue to graduate school; she hated desks. She had planned to work on that ship right up to giving birth, had dreamed of returning to it with a baby strapped to her back. Carrying the twins, and then the difficulty of keeping either of them alive, had put an end to those fancies.

"I had a friend once," her father was saying. "Used to fish with me in the summers. Excellent fisherman. Even better card player. He was good with numbers. One day he fell in love with a girl from Magnolia." Her father waved his hand derisively towards the South, where a hill reared up, its western sea-facing side graced with dignified houses. "He went to college, got a degree—fished every summer to pay for it. And then he got a job at the bank downtown. The one in the black tower. He was good at it, too, but he gave up fishing. He couldn't find the time to be on the water." Lars was scrapping something off the hull of the boat now, his face hidden.

Sigun barely managed to stifle a sigh. Her father's stories had a way of irritating her.

"I'm getting to the point, girl," he said tersely. "The point is, he loved the water, and he gave it up. He didn't fight for it, and he was miserable. Then one day, something went wrong down at the bank, and he shot himself."

Sigun dropped the piece of wood she was holding. "Dad!" She turned, looking for Erik, and spotted him up in a wooden sloop on wheels a few boats back. Not close enough to hear, he was busy talking at Tulikki, who was smiling up at him from the solid ground.

"And his wife, she was devastated. She moved up to Alaska," Lars paused to look at Sigun from under his bushy, white-gold brows. "The point is, she really did love him after all. He didn't need to be slaving away in that dark tower for her. He should have found a way to stay on the water, to stay alive. The damned idiot."

He turned back to his work. Picking up a can, he began to paint something over the scraped wood. "Got to get your feet off the land, girl. I can see it in your face."

"I was just on the ferry, wasn't I?" Her father let out a derisive scoff.

Sigun had picked up a little chisel and was testing its sharpness with her finger.

"What is it?" Lars said, straightening up to his full height and looking down at Sigun with a concerned glower.

"Nothing, really. Erik thought he saw a mermaid under the water, near Kilisut Island, and he talks about her still..."

Her father made another dismissive snort and returned to his work. "Well, when you were about his age, you declared you were going to marry a harbor seal." He let out a rumble of laughter.

"I don't remember that."

"Well, you did. You used to speak to him over the edge of the boat. He was very friendly. A big fellow. I told him he had to wait at least another twenty-five years." Her father chuckled, a deep, rough, almost uncomfortable sound. Children will imagine all sorts of things, after all, and it was a comfort to have her father dismiss her worries.

When it was time to catch the ferry home, Sigun drove Tulikki back to her little yellow house. She could see the birch tree long before they turned onto her grandmother's street. Sigun thought of mentioning the mermaid to Tulikki, but she hesitated, saying instead:

"I think Erik's swim instructor has a Finnish name." Tulikki turned to her, curious.

"What is it?"

"Merehinen."

"Merehinen," Tulikki rasped thoughtfully. "It's a little unusual, but then when people immigrate... Anyway, it's a good name for a swimmer," she laughed. "It would kind of mean a merman, you know, although maybe that would be *Vetehinen.*"

"Is that like a *näkki?*" When Sigun was just a little girl, Tulikki had taught her a charm for protection against näkki, something to say before entering the water, and the words came quickly back to her tongue: *"Näkki maalle, minä veteen,"* It was a simple charm: *näkki to the land, I to the water.* She and Tulikki would say it, tossing a stone into the sea before touching the water, like politely knocking on a door before entering a room. Tulikki had always insisted, in her lighthearted way, on reversing the spell as they left the water, to avoid angering spirits. It had been a comforting ritual in Sigun's childhood summers.

"A näkki is a little nasty thing, like a nixie," Tulikki was saying eagerly. "Always after children. You can find those tales all over. Vetehinen is an older thing. My grandmother used to say they weren't good or evil, but sea folk trapped as the land began to rise when the weight of the glaciers lifted after the last ice age. As the land rose up, bays became lakes, islands turned into peninsulas, water was separated from the sea... No one likes to feel trapped. Still, one had to be careful with them, too, so that boats wouldn't capsize, so the fishing was good, so that women weren't lured into their wild arms..."

Tulikki brushed something invisible off of her long skirt. "So maybe Merehinen would be like a Vetehinen, but one that was never caught. Or one that had escaped." She chuckled. "Anyway, it could be a Finnish name." She cast a sideways glance at Sigun. "Be careful. Don't be like your mother."

Sigun felt as if she had been slapped. "I'm not my mother." Sigun managed to keep her voice calm. Erik was in the car, after all.

"We can't help who we are," Tulikki added casually as they reached her driveway, the little yellow house glowing beneath the towering birch tree. "Think of Erik."

"That's practically all I do," retorted Sigun, her eyebrows drawn together in annoyance.

On the ferry ride home, Sigun and Erik joined the tourists on the south side of the ferry's top deck, where they were gathered to take photographs with Mount Rainier looming over the city behind them, a live volcano and one of the most dangerous in the world. Its snow-covered dome was illuminated by the warm light of the setting sun, a white-haired giant's round sleeping head nestled in the green mountains. Someone on the deck yelled excitedly "Look! Killer whales!"

Erik's feet were on the railing high above the sea, and Sigun held her body pressed against his as he leaned back into her. She pointed out over his shoulder to where four fins were slicing through the water, moving fast northwards toward the archipelago. Four bodies breached the surface, dressed in dashing black and white. Not orca whales, but *Phocoenoides dalli*, Sigun thought. A shoal of Dall's porpoises flying through the water. Sigun felt the crazy urge to dive into the sound after them, but she kept her arms wrapped around Erik, her hands curled tightly around the steel bars of the railing. Her father was right; she had been out of the water too long.

That Friday, Erik had his last swimming lesson before the start of school. He slipped into the water as happily as a duck, pushing off the side of the pool and reaching out his arms to Mr. Merehinen, who waited for him in the water.

When the lesson was over, Merehinen brought Erik back to the rim of the pool where Sigun was waiting. He stopped by the stairs, half in and half out of the water. He was looking up from the pool, and yet he managed to have the air of a king granting an audience, or a judge gazing down from his bench. When he finally spoke, he asked:

"Who is Astrid?"

"Astrid." Sigun repeated, turning away to wrap a shivering Erik in his little hooded towel, emblazoned with fire trucks. It meant something to have her daughter's name on her lips. Sigun had learned early on not to speak of her. It made people uncomfortable. Her grief frightened people. They had worried about Erik, too, but there was no reason, now, to hide her from Erik's ears. "My daughter." Sigun was toweling Erik's hair. "Erik's twin sister. Who is dead."

"I see." Mr. Merehinen considered Sigun, not with pity or compassion, exactly, and then turned to Erik. "Good work today, Erik," he said finally.

"Thank you, Mr. Merehinen," Sigun replied carefully. "For the lesson. Say thank you, Erik." Erik did, and they turned and left the man, still standing in the pool.

Sigun waited until they were home, until after lunch, until Erik was busy building.

"Did you see Astrid today?" Sigun finally asked casually. She was lying on the floor, looking up at the ceiling.

"No." He was concentrating on fitting two pieces together. "But I heard her singing under the water in the pool. She was far away, like a tickling in my ear."

Sigun closed her eyes for a moment.

"I'm learning to swim, so I can be with her." Erik added calmly.

What would a good mother do, believe him or tell him it can't be real?

Her own chest was pinched with longing to hear Astrid, to see her. Sigun imagined Astrid as a creature sewn together from the ocean itself. Eyes of sea glass, fingers made from crab legs, a heart of blood red coral. She could not bring herself to be terrified of such a daughter, even if such a daughter would have cause to be angry and jealous of the living.

Astrid, manifested or imagined, had not hurt Erik after all. It was Sigun who had been the danger to him, who had failed to keep her eyes open, as she had once failed Astrid.

On Saturday, Sigun, Tom, and Erik drove to the northern edge of the Olympic Peninsula and hiked down through the evergreen trees until they reached Dungeness Spit, a long sandy arm curling out into the water towards Victoria. They met another family with a boy and a girl close to Erik's age and the children began playing. Soon they were sharing buckets and filling them with wet sand to build a sandcastle.

Sigun knelt down beside them. "Do you want me to teach you a Finnish spell for making sandcastles? My grandmother taught it to me."

"Yes!" The girl replied, clapping her sandy hands together. Sigun glanced quickly at the girl's parents. One never knew who would be disturbed by these harmless little things, but they were talking animatedly to Tom, oblivious. Sigun helped the children tip their full buckets over. She began to tap on the bottom of a bucket with a tiny shovel and the children mimicked her, chanting:

"Älä tule paha kakku
Tule hyvä kak-ku!"

It was an order: *Don't become a bad cake, become a good cake!* They smacked the buckets in rhythm to the rhyme and, laughing, carefully lifted them to find perfectly neat sand-cakes standing proudly below. Sigun glanced up again at the boys' parents, but their mother was smiling, charmed.

The children eagerly set about filling their buckets again. Erik ran towards the surf to gather water and Sigun followed. She thought of her grandmother's charm for entering the water, but she held her tongue back, kept her lips from whispering it, just as she restrained her hand from tossing the smooth granite stone she was grasping in her palm. It was all too easy to get attached to little rituals, comforting bulwarks against the tides of fate.

Looking at Erik playing joyfully at the edge of the waves, Sigun wondered if there wasn't something cruel about ordering a creature out of the water, in removing something from its element without its consent. Anyway, she had never told Tom about the charm; he'd never heard her say it.

She glanced back at Tom, who was still speaking with the other family. The afternoon gilded his dark hair with bronze. He looked happy at a distance, painted gold by the sun, washed by the sea wind, apart from her. Free. Sigun knew her loss, her worry, her sorrow, were not hers alone. And yet, somehow the labor of keeping Erik alive felt more hers, however imperfect her skill at it.

Sigun looked back to Erik, then, just in time to see him being pulled underwater, black tentacles twisting about his legs.

"Erik!" She leapt across the sinking sand, the tide pulling at her feet. He was completely under the water now. He hadn't come back up. She could see the bright white of his striped sun shirt as he was pulled away from her, gliding west into the ocean. She lunged for him and, grabbing him around the waist, dragged him up into the air. He was too shocked to cry or even take a breath.

"Help! Tom!" Sigun screamed, but Tom was already running towards her. Long, thick rubbery strands of kelp wound around Erik. They were still pulling on his little legs as the heavy ball of kelp root rolled away on a receding wave. Sigun tore at the kelp and it tangled around her own legs. "You cannot have him!" Sigun growled at it, weeping with fury.

"Sigun," Tom said sharply, as if he had said her name many times without her hearing. He was holding Erik now, curled against his shoulder. Sigun hurled the mass of kelp roots away, far into the tide. When she turned back to Tom, he was looking at her intently over Erik's shoulder, and she could see him absorbing her words, the madness of them. She looked down, abashed. A piece of kelp was still trailing from her hand, its large floating bulb filled with gasses the alga had breathed into it. *Nereocystis luetkeana*: mermaid's bladder. She dropped it into the water as if it had scalded her hand.

On Monday, Sigun drove Erik to his pretty little preschool in the forest for the first day of school. As she watched him, he hesitated on the threshold, and looked back over his shoulder, a grave look on his face. But then he turned away to greet his teacher, and she escaped.

All summer she had been waiting for this moment when she was no longer responsible for him, when she was alone. Other parents were celebrating by going out for coffee, or rushing back to work; Sigun had a swimsuit on, hidden under her pants and an old fleece jacket.

She drove home under a gray sky heavy with clouds, and, after grabbing her bicycle, pedaled down the street toward the steep paved path that would take her through the seaside park to a remote little beach. This path was why they had chosen the house, but she had learned after moving in that a boy, out on a lark one night, had died when his bicycle had sped off it and over the cliff to the park below. Many parents moved to the island for safety, but perfect safety is impossible.

Down the treacherous path she flew, past the ruined wharf where the cormorants stood sentry as usual, brown-black and iridescent as an oil slick. When she reached the little beach, she did not use Tulikki's charm; her whole purpose was to meet whatever was in the water.

Sigun left her things on the shore and waded through the muddy shallows. Peach colored blood worms fled in frantic fringed spirals from her giant feet until it was finally deep enough to swim. The water was unbearably cold, but as she began to swim, she could no longer feel it, just the pleasure of floating in the water, the weightlessness, the grace that always came to her there.

She swam with long strong strokes out into the channel and let herself feel all of it, the longing, the grief, the anger. If some part of her daughter were there, in the dark water, lost, suspended in the old boundary between worlds, alone, vengeful even, Sigun would find her.

I love you, my daughter. Come to me. Whatever you need, take it from me.

After Erik was born, Sigun had been rushed to an operating theater by yelling doctors with shaking hands. They had tried one last time to pull Astrid out from where she had been curled beneath Sigun's heart. Sigun could feel her panicked struggle against the grasping hands before Astrid went horribly still inside her. Later, Astrid had been wheeled past Sigun, one small, perfect, plump hand lifted, waving from the bouncing speed of the trolly.

For days they had not let Sigun touch her. "She is sleeping," they had said. "She is in too much pain," they had said. Her legs had been dark with bruises. Sigun had nursed skinny, wizened Erik constantly, but she had struggled to express her scant, rich first milk into a tiny plastic cup for Astrid. The night nurse had thrown it away. "It had blood in it," she had said. As if Sigun's painful effort had spoiled the colostrum. As if a drop of her blood could contaminate what was part of her own body, her cells, her antibodies, the dissolved proteins of her tissue.

"Wake me, wake me when she is awake, even in the middle of the night," Sigun had begged. But the night nurse never had. Sigun could understand Astrid's rage because she was still full of it.

Sigun's body drifted, floating like dead wood in the channel. She had stopped shivering and her breathing slowed, as had the blood in her veins, the beat of her heart. If she drifted far enough, she would be in the path of the fast ferry to Bremerton, but she didn't lift her head to look.

Worse than the rage was the guilt. Once, when she was taking Erik to an appointment at the children's hospital, she could not help noticing the many sets of twins lurking in the waiting rooms and elevators. Twins with reconstructed skulls, twins with parents grey as ghosts, twins with tiny arms bandaged from where blood had been drawn from their little veins, their mother weeping over them as she nursed them. Sigun had not been jealous. She had thought: *I am lucky.* Even now, the guilt engulfed her, that she could feel, even for a moment, such a horrible loss to be a blessing. She thought of the ancient tales in which women leave their babies in baskets to drift on the water, or fathers abandon twins on the banks of rivers to be nursed by wolves. What if she was like them, what if she could have done more? How could Astrid ever forgive her?

I love you, my daughter. Can't you feel it? Come to me. Come for me. Take what you need from me. Devour me. I loved you.

I love you still.

Sigun felt something then, surrounding her, a longing that was hers, but not hers alone, a question. Her eyes were closed and she rested her weight on the moving sea. She nestled this presence closely to her chest. This was how it should have been, a child born in water and held over her bursting heart. She held the feeling of it, like a sea otter holds her child fast to her belly, floating on the surface of the ocean.

Just as Sigun became fearful of its end, hungry to keep it, the sense of deep communion began to release her, to leave her, to dissolve in the cold current of the channel, into the sea dark with pollution and storm water and life.

Part of Astrid was alive, after all, swimming inside Sigun's own body. Astrid's cells would live inside Sigun's blood for years, as Erik's would. To become pregnant is to become a chimera, no longer made only of yourself. Across the channel the sea lions were trumpeting again. The water was noisy with life. The sea was our first mother, and we are still made of it.

Suspended in the water and part of it, Sigun imagined she was a shapeshifter, a dragon. She was Charybdis, daughter of a sea god, a maelstrom that could capsize her family in her discontent, her anger, her sorrow, her desire. It wasn't Astrid, but she herself who was the monster. It would be easy for what was left of them to be torn apart like a brittle wooden ship into so much flotsam and jetsam, broken and scattered. It was a terrible responsibility to keep them all afloat, to keep them safe from the furious currents inside her.

A responsibility, an ability, a power that was hers alone. She would honor it. To withstand the thirsty cyclone inside her, to not allow it to swallow them up, to withstand it and to live, that would be a worthy feat of honor, a battle deserving of glory, if only in Sigun's own heart.

But Sigun had been drifting dangerously long. Her dark hair trailed out behind her in the water like the swirls of a fractal, her skin was blue with cold. The sun was somewhere up above, blanketed by the wet gray clouds. She twisted onto her belly to swim back, her eyes open wide in the dim water, but she couldn't make out the shore, and she couldn't quite feel her arms or her feet. It was as if they had vanished and she had been transformed into a salmon, silver-cheeked, bound to live forever in the watery underworld.

She felt it before she saw it, something large and fast swimming towards her beneath the slow current of the channel. Here, after all, was the sea come to claim her, Sigun thought, but her blood was so cold, her heart so slow, that she could not rise in panic. She closed her eyes instead.

Only when arms wrapped around her did she realize the animal swimming towards her had not been a whale or a seal or a shark, but a man, who rolled her onto her back and lifted her head out of the water. She was pressed by the gentle waves against his body, his black wetsuit as slick and velvety as seal skin. He pushed his diving mask up into his silver hair: Mr. Merehinen.

She noticed that his eyes were not actually green, but a cold storm grey, the pupils rimmed with a halo of gold, like the last glimmer of the sun on the crest of a winter sea.

"Sigun! You are alive." It came across not as a question, or statement even, but a stern command. His deep voice shivered across the calm water.

When she made no move to escape, he embraced her, one arm curled beneath her knees and the other wrapped around her chest right below her left breast, holding her to his chest. As they reached shallow water, he picked her up out of the water easily and carried her as if she were still weightless, despite the awkward neoprene mittens that hid his hands, the flippers on his feet, which slapped in the shallow water of the muddy beach.

"Yes, I am. I am alive, thank you," Sigun said, or she thought she said, her lips were still blue with cold. She was filled with gratitude, and she felt as if she could have left her forehead on his shoulder forever, but it wasn't only solace she felt.

She wriggled from his arms like a fish, and stood, towering over him.

He stood very still, his chin up as he contemplated her. There was a quality to his stillness that was transfixing. His attention was so focused on her that Sigun felt heat flood her cheeks. She was blushing and she was so surprised to feel it, she found it so delightfully mortifying, that she had to stifle a chuckle of mirth. Instead, she lowered her eyes, in an attempt to appear demure, remembering her grandmother's rules of etiquette when encountering strange creatures in the forest, unsettling men in parks, animals rising out of wild water: to be respectful and polite, to move away quickly.

"I could help you," his voice was quiet now, a low whisper, "to learn to swim in this water. If you want."

"Not today, but thank you, Mr. Merehinen." Her cheeks flaming, she risked one last fleeting look at his face and was almost sure she saw a flicker of expression there, that his eyes were crinkled at the edges with amusement, that the golden rings around his dilated pupils glowed. Sigun turned, hurriedly towards her bicycle, careful not to chance even a glance over her shoulder. Her skin was still blue with cold, but she felt remarkably revived.

When she finally reached it, Sigun leapt onto her bicycle and raced back through the park, past the old wharf, now empty of cormorants except for the one, streaked red with blood, vanquished below the talons of a bald eagle that was piercing the midday with its incongruously beautiful cry. She hurtled up the treacherous path, pedaling ferociously, her blood (Astrid's blood, Erik's blood) heating again, her lungs burning, to where her house perched precariously on the steep hillside above the water.

Grief is not something that can be nailed in a wooden box and buried, and neither is desire. They ebb and flow like the tide; one has to learn to navigate them. There is no perfect closure, and to believe in one would be a perilous delusion, a mirage, like an island of perfect safety, a sea without monsters.

She sped, cutting off from the paved road and bouncing down the short-cut through the woods where blackberry branches stretched out across a dirt path with monstrous, spiny arms that lashed her bare skin and pinged against the spokes of her furiously spinning wheels.

The air was heavy with the sweet ferment of August berries as Sigun burst out of the forest onto to her ordinary, paved street lined with houses. As she put her hand on the door latch, it opened from within, and Tom was standing on the threshold.

"I left the office early—I wanted to go with you to pick up Erik..." His eyes wandered over her, taking in her red cheeks and the cold, blue skin of her arms, the seaweed in her hair, the hermit crab clinging, terrified, to her swimsuit, which was all she was wearing. She had left her clothes at the beach. He lifted a hand out towards her, gently removing the hermit crab and placing it aside.

She raised her eyes to his face, unsure of what she would find there. At some point, Sigun had lost her confidence that Tom could know her and still love her, let alone want her as she stood now, her hair beribboned with seaweed, her arms red with scratches and tiny drops of blood from the pricks of the blackberry brambles. Sigun thought suddenly of what must have been the exact moment she had fallen in love with him. It was soon after they had met and she had taken him out sailing in one of her father's boats. Tom hadn't grown up around the water, and he was awkward in a boat. She should have been careful with him, but she was overjoyed to be out on the sea again. The wind was strong that day, and had picked up even further to a fierce gale. Sigun hadn't been able to hold back, and she had been laughing as they ran with the wind, the spray of the water hitting her young, grinning face. She had looked back at him in her wild joy, suddenly unsure of what she would find. He was seeing her in her element, unrestrained in all her terrible power and glory, but he met her eyes, not with terror or anger, but admiration. He had trusted her, putting his life in her hands as they flew over the water.

Now, Tom smiled down at her from the front step, with wary affection and longing in his eyes. "You look like yourself again," he said.

"I feel alive again," Sigun said and she found herself grinning back at him. She took his warm, dry hand in her cold, salty one, and placed it over the cool damp skin above her heart. "I don't want to be late to pick up Erik," she said, "But I need to warm up before we go..." Then Tom was pulling her through the door and Sigun was pushing the door shut. They were laughing as they raced up the stairs, her long arm wrapped around his and their hands tangled together.

Sigun's skin tingled almost painfully as her heated blood flowed into the last edges of her body, flushed to the tips of her fingers. She could feel everything again and the return of feeling was a stinging effervescence. She was a pulsing medusa, venomous, bioluminescent, ephemeral. Sigun could feel in that moment, haunted and monstrous though she might be, not only the anguish of living, but also the joy and pleasure of it. She could feel the triumph and the fragility of it, the grace and good fortune of being there, terribly, magnificently alive.

See J.J. Eskelin's story "Astrid Underwater"
online at Metaphorosis.
If you liked it, leave a comment. Authors love
that!
Remember to subscribe to our e-mail updates so
you'll know when new stories are posted.

About the story

When I embarked upon writing "Astrid Underwater", I did not set out to make a story that drew upon Finnish art and myth, but as it evolved, Finnish myth bubbled up in to it. In the story, there is an exhibit of paintings by Akseli Gallen-Kallela. His images of Finnish myth are among the most iconic. Years ago, I used to live near his house, a little Jugend castle on a bluff above the sea, and once I even went to a smoke sauna in his turf-covered sauna, an ancient building, older than the house and built into the hillside on the shore of Laajalahti. However famous he is in Finland, I don't think Gallen-Kallela has ever had a major exhibit in the United States, at least not in my memory. At one point, I thought I should take his paintings out of the story altogether, but I couldn't bear to do it. There was this resonance, not only with his work as I went back to look again, but with the myths underlying it. That resonance kept me going when this story was unruly and difficult. It was the blood running underneath the bones of the story. However, the most unexpected thing to me was that, as I was challenged to go deeper through the editing process, how I saw his work, and my relationship to the underlying myths was transformed. One of the last things I added to the story was Sigun looking at Gallen-Kallela's painting of Louhi. In the Kalevala, Louhi is the chief antagonist, a frightening woman with magical powers. She is also a fiercely protective mother. The juxtaposition of Louhi and Sigun felt like something I had been missing all along. Seeing Louhi through Sigun's gaze, my own interpretation of her was altered. Now, when I look at

Louhi, a hostile monster hovering above the boat that is stealing away her treasure, I see her differently; I hope she wins.

A question for the author

Q: Do you generally start with mood, title, character, concept...?

A: When I start to work on a particular idea in earnest, it is because I have a strong feeling about it. I often feel a sense of urgency to capture it, to try to convey a particular image or scene, a voice. If it is an idea that has been haunting me for a while, I will have a clear concept of the beginning and the end. Even so, there is usually something I only uncover as it develops, some underlying secret that surprises me. To help evoke the particular feeling of a story, the texture and sensation of a particular piece, I have started to write out every word I can think of that captures the feeling I am trying to communicate. I write these not as a list, but by hand as a free-form, organic, cloud of words. Maybe this sounds silly, but sometimes I see something there I have been missing; something I have been struggling grasp rises to the surface. Writing for me can be like being caught up in a wave. I won't pretend to have a great control of my process; I am still learning to find a way to let my subconscious do its work, and to not be afraid of the outcome.

About the author

J.J. Eskelin is a writer of speculative fiction currently living with her family on the Central Coast of California. She has lived in Finland, England, and the United States, and is a dual Finnish and American citizen. Nature and place are important to her, and, no matter where she is, she tries to escape with her giant dog to commune with wilderness on a weekly basis.

jjeskelin.com

She Was the Universe

Damian Stockli

Feb. 1st, 2030

Night shift in the facility always began the same.

Arni woke at 7:00 PM, on the temper foam mattress that had once belonged to Governor Björnsson. He used the governor's shower, his electric toothbrush, and the wool clothes hot from his personal laundry machine—Björnsson wasn't there to protest, was he?—and finally clicked his watch into place. Shower-teeth-shirt-pants-watch, in that order, every night, invariably. The final item of the routine was in the bottom drawer, hidden in a wad of socks: the diamond ring, from when Arni's parents were in love. He pushed it deep into his pocket.

At breakfast, the empty cafeteria echoed with every spoon clink of his Rice Chex and soy milk. Arni explored the grooves of the diamond as he ate. It wasn't fashionable to propose in your twenties, not in Iceland, but Arni had no illusions about it. It was a sure thing, and he needed a sure thing. She would understand.

"So this is, potentially, a kind of stupid question. A potentially, a kind of, a— No."

After breakfast was hydroponics work: managing nutrient levels in the soil, testing to ensure the fungal infection in their wheat didn't escape its quarantined cell. Every time he looked down at the floor, he imagined the ring falling between the bars of the plastic grate and getting lost in the irrigation pipes. *Mamma* had given it to him when he was eleven, after his father had taken a head-on collision along Route 41. She'd said one day he'd make his own home with it. He was careful to keep his free hand cupped over the right pant pocket.

"I figured this is a sure thing. We could all use a sure thing, in times like— No."

Tests came out negative. Plants healthy.

At 10:00 PM, Arni jogged the long way around the facility to reach the south exit. The quiet corridors exploded with the sort of high art graffiti he used to see in Reykjavík: a small girl reading a book under a maple tree, a family of magic tortoises, a woman's hair folding into ocean waves. Good exercise, good view, and it was best to avoid the dormitories, so Arni took the long way every night, invariably.

"Is it open season for—? Siggi, can I ask you a real—? Ugh, Christ."

He nabbed some of their industrial-grade salve at the worker's closet, then thought about Siggi as he applied it to the cold-cracked skin of his hands. It wasn't fashionable to propose in your twenties, but who was around to judge them now? On went two more layers of wool and polypropylene so not a square centimeter of his skin was exposed to the air. Still his nose hairs went solid as he rotated the exterior lock. He hiked up his neck-buff.

It was a clear night, the Reykjanes basalt frosted over and glimmering with starlight. Arni retraced the path of a thousand frozen footsteps from the shelter to the power plant. The blood returned to his face on the way inside, where he resumed his role as one-man control room operation and maintenance crew. Most of the night was spent monitoring corrosion in the injection wells, doing freedom tests on the stop valves, and, when necessary, stepping into the wide turbine room for visual checkups and mechanical repair. Tonight he noticed a single aberration in a control valve's response time, but it didn't persist.

6:00 AM—there always comes a time to put the work down and go home, *Mamma* had said.

But not quite yet.

Arni suited up and spun the exterior lock. The silhouette of the old Reykjanes lighthouse cut a dark thumb out of the starry horizon, and that was his guide to the shore. He didn't look at Jonas's corpse, frozen stuck along his path. When he reached the shore, he plopped onto the ice-crusted ground under a million stars. Each night Arni marveled at the galactic disk, arching horizon to horizon like spilled cosmic milk. The black background of space only appeared as cracks in the light.

He slid his hand between his layers, searching for the pocket. When he found the ring, it looked baby-sized in his double-gloved hand.

"Hey, um, Siggi. There's...." His voice was hoarse. "I have something I need to tell you."

No. Siggi wouldn't be charmed by theatrics. He would have to try harder, be a little more original.

He cleared his throat. "Is it open season for stupid questions? Because I have... one... Fuck. So, is it open season for stupid questions?" He huffed through his neck-buff. "You sound like an asshole, Arni."

He found a more comfortable position, sat up. Chest out, right? Confidence. "Okay.... Hey, Siggi, so, can I be serious with you for a second? I have to say something, and it has to do with something I sensed you weren't too keen on in the past, but I guess I figured, maybe, this was... maybe—"

Arni let himself fall back onto the ice. "Shit."

He figured he'd get it before the sun rose.

Aug. 6th, 2026

"I'm just trying to get you out of that, y'know, that *place*," said Erik, gesturing to the opposite end of the bar. "This could be something good for you. It's been a year, man. Live."

Arni peered left halfway through a swig. The bar was circular, in the middle of the place, so a row of Svedka was just eclipsing her face. She was mixing a drink while she talked up Júlia and Helga. "I have a lot of good things," said Arni. "My therapist has me keep a gratitude journal now."

The trio was framed against a wall of paintings—a nude woman on a beach, a weary fisherman with shining boots, a wintery village. Last week, she had had him guess which was hers, and he got it on the nineteenth try: the little girl reading under a big red maple. She had given him a print of it after, and when he got home he put it in a drawer and not on the wall, because he thought that would be creepy.

The volume of Erik's groans usually depended on how many drinks he'd had. Tonight he'd had quite a few. "I'm not talkin' about job, I'm not talkin' about mortgage, I'm talkin' about *living*, Arnar."

"Don't call me that."

"What? *Arnar?* You only get to be happy Arni once you're living again."

It was an unusually lively weeknight at the Ölstofa, and the scene was beginning to wear Arni down. He had hoped to drink quietly and watch the news for developments on the story going around the water cooler. He hadn't anticipated everyone would be there for the same thing, laughing and cursing each other out and building stacks of cash at the bar and every table. Through a jumble of bobbing heads, he saw the image on TV. It was a true-color reading from the Hawaii observatory, showing an elongated blue-white flare on a background of stars. The 'alien thing' was getting a name tonight, and three options appeared in a list: *Eos, Shamash, Phaeton.* Everyone had a bet.

"You two doing okay over here?!"

Arni froze. Sleeves rolled up, freckles and a silver ponytail. Her name, *Sigrún,* was sewn into her shirt in cursive lettering.

"Just giving my friend a little therapy!" said Erik, over the noise.

She grinned, shining a glass. "Parents fucked you up, huh?"

Arni's head got heavy.

"… sorry, did I say something?" she asked.

Erik waved the concern away. "He's just getting over something. Don't—how about this? What do you think about the alien thing? We're definitely gettin' invaded, right?"

" 'Present fears are less than horrible imaginings'," she said, in practiced English. "But hey, I want to know what the science guy thinks." She pointed to the stitching on Arni's own work uniform: *Arnar Ívarsson | Reykjanes Power Station | Mechanical Engineer.*

He laughed. "Caught me."

"What's the prognosis, then?"

"Well, it's on a heliacal vector, so it's probably going to burn up or get captured by the sun's gravity. As for whether it's aliens…"

"*All*-right, this is where I check out," Erik said, giving Arni one last squeeze on the shoulder. "You two have fun with this gripping conversation." He slid through the forest of bodies then took a seat by Júlia, who beamed and hugged him.

Arni sighed. "Sorry. Are you actually interested in this?"

Sigrún shrugged, but didn't break eye contact.

"Okay. So, it's a high velocity object of extrasolar origin. That's what we know. Aliens are always the last hypothesis."

"Always. Of course."

"But the cool thing is the ionized particles making the light. See, that's not what comet dust looks like. And the reason people are *saying* aliens is because there's a hypothesis going around that it's the effects of a fusion—"

A curse split the noise, commanding everybody to quiet. The whole bar shushed and turned to the anchor on TV. The suit looked down at his tablet, and drew out the last word of each sentence: "The votes are innn... Here we gooo... and the name, is..."—a pause for optimal effect —"Phaeton!" The noise around them swelled to a pitch, and the stacks of cash were distributed appropriately. Erik, apparently a winner, fanned his face with bills and pretended to faint into Júlia's arms. Laughs all around.

"Get another drink out of him while he's feeling gracious," said Sigrún.

"Eh, some of us need to work tomorrow," said Arni, pointing to the stitching in his shirt.

"Don't I know it. But he's right, I think you could live a little," she said. She was juggling the conversation with another order now. "You only get away with the brooding because you're cute, and that won't last forever, Arnar."

His stomach sank. Her eyes bored straight through him. "You—you heard?"

"You get good ears in this business," she said, filling a glass with the house brew. "But listen. It sounds like you're getting over a breakup, and I'm not handing out rebounds."

"My mother died."

Sigrún handed the patron his drink, then froze. She didn't look back at him. "Sorry," she mouthed, too quiet to hear over the noise.

"You couldn't know," he shouted. "It's okay. I'm in therapy and all that." The regret was burning in his forehand. He searched for a way back. "But listen. I'm warning you now that my power plant salary isn't as high as most people think, if that's your angle."

"Curses, foiled again," she said. "Do you want to start this conversation from the beginning, Arnar?"

A familiar rush snuck up on him. Something good? "Call me Arni," he said, pointing to the stitching in his shirt.

"Siggi," she said, pointing to her own.

"So what are you up to tomorrow night?"

Siggi's smile widened like light breaking. "Mondays are better for me."

Feb. 2nd, 2030

7:00 PM on the governor's bed.

Arni washed and brushed. He grabbed the ring from the drawer and slipped it in his pocket.

He ate his Rice Chex in soy milk.

And tended to the crops in hydroponics.

He avoided the dormitories.

An eventful night at the plant. The faulty control valve had failed to trip while he was gone, so the turbine was spinning so fast it would disassemble within hours. Arni unhoused the valve actuator to work on it, steam piping into the turbine room. When the valve shot closed on his left pinky and ring fingers, he discovered it was an electrical hiccup in the governing mechanism, not the actuator itself. His team would have stopped him from making the assumption, if they were there.

He flipped the emergency release and pulled his fingers out of the steam, ignored the swelling and burns, fixed the electrical bug, then proceeded to the shore.

Ring in his hand.

"Is it a cliche to say you make everything worth it?"

Jan. 31st, 2027

When Arni was six years old, his father had dug a hole in their backyard after they found hot groundwater breaking the surface there. They had let the water fill the hole, and set up a rain gutter to let it run down the hill. The empty house was for vacation now, so when they made the trip out he insisted Siggi give their manmade hot spring a try.

Phaeton-3, the third object of its kind, happened to cross Earth's orbit close enough to be visible in the northern hemisphere in daytime. With his face just above the water, Arni watched the pale white streak in the sky.

Siggi, slowly floating from the opposite end, finally collided with his arm.

"What are you thinking?" he said, to break the quiet. "You okay?"

"Every time you ask me that, do you think this will finally be where I say I'm leaving you?"

"It's a habit, isn't it?"

" 'Words like violence, break the silence. Come crashing in. Into my little world.' "

"More English poetry?"

"Yes."

"Ah."

"So what are *you* thinking, *elskan mín*?"

A cloud passed over the white streak, and a gust of wind nipped Arni's nose. "That coming back to this house is easier with you. It's funny. *Pabbi* used to joke that I'd bring a girl here one day."

She frowned. "You haven't told me much about him."

Arni shook his head. "He was here until I was eleven, and then a car accident. It's old news, really. But at the time, it... I don't know. It's like it broke the world."

"Only tell me what you want."

A world of memories broke the surface. He pushed them out. "The thing I remember most was my mother. I couldn't let her leave my sight after that. It was like... Schrödinger's *Mamma*. Ugh, God she'd slap me for that one."

"What do you mean?"

"Every time she left the room, she could be gone. I just couldn't... *not know*. I had to *know*. That she was still there. Does that make sense? So I had problems going in to school. For a year, I went in late or I didn't go at all. They sent me work to do at home when I could, and the only subject I stayed ahead in was math." He laughed. "There's always an answer in math, right?"

"Including a financial answer, which you of course have found as well."

"Yes," he chuckled. "I was attached to her for a long time. And a year ago I finally lost her too, and this house went empty. Orphaned, at twenty-five. Whenever I pull in the driveway, it feels like she'll stick her head out the front door."

She frowned. "I'm sorry, *elskan*."

"But it wasn't as much a shock as *Pabbi*, you know? *Mamma* had MS for years, even when he was alive. I think it's uncertainty that gets me. I can't not know what's going to happen next."

Siggi sat up, staring at the clouds with sullen eyes. "I think I'm the opposite way."

"Really?"

"People on this island," she looked at him with that stare, "settle into lives early. I think that's like death. When nothing changes, when you know everything that's coming at you. It sounds crazy, but dying in bed at 90 scares me. Knowing that I could get shot tomorrow? That helps me sleep. Because I know it's not all going one place."

"So you wouldn't grow old with me?"

She tilted her head. "Arnar. Come on."

He let his head fall back into the water, and watched the clouds drift past the snowy edge of the hole. Siggi placed her wet hand on his chest, and her face appeared above him, eyes now gone soft. "Just answer me this," she said. "Am I the girl you were always supposed to bring here, or am I me?"

"I don't understand."

"She was a vision your father created. Am I her, or am I me?"

"Of course you're you."

With a smirk, she said, "Don't forget it," then held her nose and went under the water again.

Feb. 3rd, 2030
Wake up at 7:00 PM.
Get dressed. Grab ring.
Breakfast.
Make sure the crops are healthy.
Avoid the dormitories.
Can no longer ignore burns and swelling in fingers. Probably broken. Apply topical ointment and splint.
Work at the plant.
Pass the corpse. See the stars.
The ring.
"I asked you once if you'd grow old with me. Now I have a sequel to that question."

Aug. 30th, 2028
"Is it competition on the job market?" she asked, looking down at him in his spot at the kitchen table. "Is that the problem?"
"No, no."
"Is it English? Are you afraid of having to use English for your job?"
"My English is... fine."

A letter had shown up in their mailbox a week prior—Siggi's fellowship. They were both ecstatic at its arrival. Only now was he losing his footing. Siggi had cleared the books from her desk, and the letter had sat there since. Arni found himself avoiding it.

"London is going to be harder than Reykjavík, I know that, but from everything you tell me, you're good at what you do and your position is *in demand.* In my field, I can't just pitch a tent wherever I want in the developed world. You can."

"Siggi, the industry is more complicated than that."

She drew out a long breath. "Don't pull that with me. You know I know what's what."

"Can we just give this more time? Maybe we're not ready for that yet."

"That's..." Another breath. "That's not how a fellowship works, Arni. I can't defer forever. I'm..." She looked down at her empty palms, then up at him. The stare. "I'm trying to make *this* work right now."

"What if we end up there forever?"

"What is keeping you *here*? God help me, I'm struggling to figure out *what* is keeping you here. Do you have *anything* here?”

"Really? You're going there?”

"Oh, Arni. You know that's not what I mean.”

"Then what do you mean?”

"Arni...” She glanced out the window, drawing another breath, but it came staggered. "I love you, but I have to take this.” She rubbed something out of her eyes. "And because I love you, I don't want this to be an ultimatum.”

He shook his head. "I don't know that word.”

"A final decision.”

"It feels like that's what this is.”

"I can't—” she said, hands in her face. "I'm bad at this.” She grabbed her jacket from a kitchen chair. Then she snagged her keys from the counter. Arni was standing before he realized it. *Where are you going?* he would have said next, but she read it on his face. His face gave everything away, she always said. "I'm going to my family's house. I'm not punishing you, I just... I just need to think, I want you to think too, okay? I'll see you tomorrow. Okay? Okay.”

There was a *creeaak-BANG* on the door, then quiet. Arni was alone again.

Feb 4th, 2030
   7:00 PM.
   Grab the ring.
   Work.
   Avoid the dormitories.
   Burns not healing. Discoloration. Possibly exposure to cold.
   Sit on the shore anyway.
   The ring.
   "You always say the only constant is change. What about one more constant? Just one more?"

Sep. 30th, 2028
   Arni's feet were propped on the ottoman, silhouetted against the TV screen. A sharp ache stabbed at his knees, since his legs had no support, but he didn't dare move them. Siggi had fallen asleep with her head in his lap. She smelled like alcohol and bar food. Her bare feet were at the edge of the couch, veins bulging, bright red blisters around her ankles. Arni held her acceptance letter

in his right hand, stroked her hair in his left.

The TV made its noise: "This marks the *thirty-ninth* object that has entered our solar system since last year. Astronomers expect Phaeton-39 to follow a similar pattern to each one that has come before it, being captured by the sun's gravity and entering a low-solar orbit. We'll continue to provide updates..."

Arni placed the letter by his feet, then remembered, in *Mamma* and *Pabbi*'s house, the ring in the bottom left drawer of their dresser.

Feb. 5th, 2030
    7:00 PM.
    Ring.
    Work.
    Avoid the dormitories.
    Burns still not healing. Dark purple.
    Jonas is really frozen solid.
    Ring.
    "There's just something I need to get off my chest. And I promised myself I'd do it."

Nov. 4th, 2028

Tonight was the night.

On the old king bed in his parents' house, Arni laid two tickets to London Heathrow International—and their diamond ring. "You're going to ask her before the sun rises. She'll say yes. You make your—It'll be fine. Fine." He dropped both into his jacket pocket and spritzed himself with cologne.

The plan was dinner on the back deck. The food was almost out of the oven, the table was set, and the night was clear. The aurorae borealis were out in a flood, jittery green ribbons being towed across the sky from some uncertain point beyond the mountains. There was a soft green glow on the deck and table setting. Nature had been kind to him.

Siggi pulled into the driveway at 7:00, looking confused by his outfit. "Should I have worn my work uniform?"

"No need, since I'm waiting on you today. Come out back."

She reacted with the surprise he was hoping for, but there was a sense of urgency underneath which—he thought—they could both feel. It was all a romantic gesture, but she must have wondered, and he knew she must have wondered:

Why? Before carting out the wine, he told her he had something for her. She was still smiling when her brow furrowed, but when he reached into his jacket, and told her to close her eyes, she frowned. In that second while her eyes were closed, he thought he might have guessed what her answer would be.

"You can open."

When she saw the boarding passes spread on the table, her shoulders relaxed. She put on a happy frown, and met his eyes. "Thank you, *elskan mín.*"

"Call it the appetizer. Now, the rest!"

The night ran away from there. They talked about the old days at the bar, Erik and Júlia's on/off relationship, Arni's obsessive boss, and of course, the life that waited for them in England. He admitted to her he was scared, and he was going to need to brush up his English, but he wanted the best for her. They were going to make a new life.

When the meal was finished they took their clothes off and went back to the spring Arni's father had dug. He kept the ring balled in a tight fist under the water as they floated and watched the aurorae in the sky, green glow scattering off the surface and lighting her face.

"Siggi."

She kept her eyes on the sky. "Yeah?"

So you wouldn't grow old with me?

He felt the hard diamond between his fingers. If he squeezed tighter he'd bleed. "Siggi, I need to ask you someth—"

"Wait. *Elskan,* have you seen this before? The sky."

The aurorae all seemed to thin at once. First, the accents of blue and violet at the upper edges dissipated. Then he watched as the green glow in the water around Siggi dimmed. "No," he said. "Never in my life."

The ribbons, all the way to their origin beyond the mountains, dimmed until they were gone. The moon's face shifted, gradually, from its bright white to a dull gray, and they watched it until it too dimmed into a black disk. Then the stars came out. A thousand new points of light broke through and twinkled all at once, more than he had seen in his life. The black of space became cracks in the light.

"What just happened?" she said.

He tightened his fist around the ring. "I don't know."

Feb. 6th, 2030
Ring.
Avoid the dormitories.
Amputated fingers.
Shore.
Ring.
"You knew it was coming."

Nov. 6th, 2028
Arni took a dixie cup from the water cooler back to his desk, and stared at the clock on the control room wall. He'd give himself ten minutes to zone out—what passed for a break now—and then he'd go back into the meeting with Magnús and Anna and the rest. He was on his fourteenth hour and third energy drink. His team had never been this busy before.

The clock: 6:59 PM.

Two days. 48 hours. The night had lasted 48 hours. The banality of it was unsettling, but also misleading. The lights in their houses still worked. Their electricity and plumbing was still there. Cars still had gas. The internet worked. As far as anybody could tell, they had entered eternal night, and that was it. It was just sustained darkness. Arni knew better.

He did the math.

1 day: avg. global temp 14 degrees C, immediate cessation of photosynthesis worldwide, lives lost negligible

7 days: global avg. temp 0 degrees C, all grass and cereals dead, halted supply chains ~10 million lives lost

30 days: global avg. temp -30 degrees C, complete ecological collapse as scavenger species die off (cats in Reykjavík), emergency stockpiles near depletion, ~5.4 billion lives lost

365 days: global avg. temp -75 degrees C, frozen oceans, long-range radio comm unusable due to ionosphere deterioration, only people left are who we manage to save

4,000 days: global avg. temp -130 degrees C, air begins to condense into snow, shielding required on facilities to protect survivors from exposure to cosmic radiation

7:09 PM. Break over.

Arni's watch read 7:08—a minute slower than the control room's atomic clock. He twisted the minute-hand a hair forward, then wound it. Only seven minutes later, he found himself winding it again.

Feb. 7th, 2030
   Ring.
   Three frostbitten toes amputated.
   Shore.
   Ring.
   "With a thick enough jacket, we could ice-skate to anywhere in the world now. Ha. How does that sound?"

Dec. 1st, 2028
   "Sir, you're not priority," the guard said to Erik, his breath a white fog.
   "What the fuck does that mean?" said Júlia. She stuck an arm out toward Siggi and Arni. "We're their friends. You have to."
   The guns had finally come out. Route 425 was barricaded a mile and a half out from the plant. Just behind Erik and Júlia, cars on both lanes, backed up all the way to the airport. Somehow the word had spread. Things were getting tense under the stars.

"Why can't they come?" said Siggi.

"Mr. Ívarsson is priority, and you're his plus one. We're at capacity until more of the shelter is constructed."

"They'll take you on the next round," Arni said to his friends. They looked between him and the guard, bundled under blankets, fear-stricken. "They will."

"You're sure?" said Erik.

"I'll see you soon," said Arni.

"O— Okay," said Erik.

"Okay," said Júlia.

The guards pushed Erik and Júlia back with the rest of the bundled squatters along the road. Arni put his hand on Siggi's back and they walked together to the shuttle bus, windows glowing yellow in the darkness. When Arni looked back, Erik was still watching him go.

"They're going to get in, right?" said Siggi.

Arni stuck his hands in his pockets and shivered.

"Arnar, they're going to get in, right?"

Feb. 8th, 2030
Ring.

Avoid the dormitories.
Shore.
Ring.
"You've read my mind plenty before, haven't you?"

Dec. 21st, 2028

Anna, now a project lead, scribbled the equation on a napkin and shoved it in his face. "Negative sixty-two celsius: with only one jacket that's hypothermia for you in under ten minutes. Remember Jonas? There will be no more dead engineers on this team. Put. On. Your. Jacket."

"There's no time."

"Mr. Íva—"

"No time. I need to get the modified fuel to—"

"You have time to put on your jacket, Mr. Ívarsson. You do not have time to argue with me."

Feb. 9th, 2030

Ring.
Avoid the dormitories.
Ring.

Take as long as you want, elskan.

Oct. 3rd, 2029

The walls of their shelter were made with an ICF process modified for insulation in subarctic temperatures. The interior-facing polystyrene blocks were sheeted with fiberglass paneling cannibalized from the state building and other power plants, making hallways of hospital white gloss. This was a problem Siggi had led the initiative to fix. When Arni walked to the south exit for work in the plant each day, the halls were covered in springtime vistas, psychedelic cascades, and animals the children had done.

In Dormitory 02-02, Arni and Siggi's Sistine Chapel, two plane tickets were wedged in the frame of a wall mirror. The plaster walls and ceiling had become a baroque sky-scape, the circular mirror its rising sun emanating light beams. Siggi dabbed her brush with more yellow, and dashed a beam with definition, carefully avoiding the tickets. Arni lay in bed, mesmerized by the precision of each brushstroke.

Siggi mumbled as she flicked her brush. "Tyson sphere? Dagursson sphere? *Dyson* sphere." Then, in her soft English: " 'Darkness had no need of aid from them—she was the universe.' "

Feb. 10th, 2030
Avoid the dormitories.
Ring.
Schrödinger's dormitories? Ha.

Nov. 21st, 2029
Sitting at his terminal, Magnús sent a diagnostic request to master control, and it produced pages of text in less than a minute. Arni and each person on the control team read it individually, then gave Magnús the okay. He sent in another diagnostic request, and the same process followed. They repeated this action at least five times. When it was clear that the plant would stay in perfect shape for at least another 24 hours, Magnús stood at the front of the room. He took a deep breath.

"Alright everybody, good work. Before we… close the book… on this place, I just want you to know how proud I am of all of you. I don't want a single one of you to think that we failed here. Maybe we can't say the same for the botanists…"

Weak laughter.

"… but the engineering staff… You did what shouldn't have been possible. I especially want to recognize Arni Ívarsson and Anna Jónsdottir for their work developing the conduction system running from the plant to the shelter. We were lucky enough to have Iceland. But we were even luckier to have Arni and Anna on our team. Your work was a godsend."

Lucky to have Iceland. The geothermal vents were their salvation. Everyone with the means had drafted plans for nuclear powered bunkers, but couldn't stay ahead of the chaos. On the newscasts around the world they had seen many bright orange flashes in the darkness die slowly and give way to the starlight. The radio signals had gone one by one, the last a persistent communication from Nishiyama, just lost a month and a half ago with the last of the planet's ionosphere. Iceland might have been the last man standing.

Even then, a blight in their hydroponics had gotten them. There'd been no genetic diversity in their fruit and cereal farms. The fungus tore right through one cell, then leaked into the irrigation pipes and took out the rest. Dr. Gunnarsson had led an expedition to the Svalbard Seed Vault to prevent that very thing from happening, but found that the E.U. people had already stolen the seeds and taken them back to Germany. Some good it had done them.

The engineering team suited up under all three layers, then Magnús led them across the ice to the shelter for the last time. Arni and Anna walked together in silence.

"Did you tell your husband about... you know, the dinner tonight?" he asked.

Anna shook her head.

"It doesn't feel right," he said, "making this decision for everyone. I don't know."

"With Kristján..." said Anna. "He'll fight to the end. But that's exactly why. It's just better that some people don't know."

"Yeah," he said.

"But you told Siggi about the dinner?"

"Yeah," he said. "She— It just— I knew... that she'd want to know."

Anna put a comforting hand on his back. "All good things, Arni, all good things. Take one more look at the stars before we go in."

There they were, like always, fixed. At the end of the night, maybe the humans would be gone, but the earth would keep turning, and they'd still shine down, and all of it would keep on moving like they never existed in the first place. There was an interesting feeling there. If he asked Siggi, she could probably cite a poem or a painting or a book about it. He wished he had had the time to read them.

"Don't feel humbled by them," said Anna. "A few trillion years, and they burn out too. The little green guys that stole the sun? Don't know what they're gonna do then. It all trends toward stasis. We just made it to the Big Freeze a little early." She nudged his shoulder. "Like ants who nested in some nice-looking lumber."

He wasn't sure how the idea gave Anna peace. As she took in the stars, he didn't see fear on her face. For the rest of the night, right up until the last moment he saw her, none.

Arni helped prepare the last supper, but he and Siggi didn't eat, knowing what they knew. Most of the facility's inhabitants weren't clued in as to why Governor Björnsson had called for a feast so large it nearly depleted their store of luxury food, but they didn't question it. The people were hungry, many of them emaciated. Some of the youngest children had swollen bellies, a mark of protein deficiency. Until three months ago, Arni had never seen children that looked like that with his own eyes. The facility's main cafeteria echoed with thousands of happy voices. A sadness pulled him down as he watched them all devour their food, but this was better than starvation—and the violence that accompanied it. The governor had made the right call. He was tearing into a steak not twenty feet away.

The night came to an end when a profound tiredness fell on all 5,402 Iceland survivors. Each cafeteria was cleaned, and everybody shuffled through the corridors to go sleep.

Around 10:00 PM, in their tiny unit, Arni sat on the edge of his bed with Siggi. Had the light been turned on, he might have gotten a look at their Sistine sky, but only a thin bar emanated below the door. Siggi was gaunt and fragile, her freckled cheeks sunken, the silver color in her hair now only down to the tips. He wondered if that meant the Siggi he knew was gone away, or if this was who she always was, underneath, waiting to come out. He wondered that about everybody.

Her hand felt like a vice around his. He thought she might have been scared.

The ring was in his pocket, still there, waiting.

She kissed him. "I love you."

"I love you."

She produced two capsules of pentobarbital. He could have mistaken them for multivitamins, or antibiotics. "Are you ready, *elskan mín*?"

But the ring.

He cupped his hands over them. "What if we didn't?"

She looked sad. "Arni..."

"I know there's one hydroponic cell left. I know that's enough to sustain five people for life, and I know I can maintain it *and* the plant alone if I need to. It won't keep the species alive, but it'll keep us alive. It would just be us. It could work. I know it."

"Arni... That won't be living."

But the ring. What about the ring?

"Stay here with me," said Siggi. "Please."

It wasn't supposed to go like this.

"Okay," he said.

A smile. A kiss. She pulled his hand off and slid the pill into her mouth. He did the same.

Siggi swallowed.

Arni felt the capsule roll around on the roof of his mouth, but he couldn't push the thing back. It wouldn't work. Something in his mind, his jaw, his tongue—it wouldn't let him do it. The pill stayed there, even as she fell into bed with him and brought the sheets over. He held her bony head to his chest.

The ring. In his pocket.

"Siggi?"

"I'm here, *elskan*."

"I— I— I have to— I..."

"Shh. Stay with me. It's okay."

The mean pill sat there, pressed between tongue and gums. The not knowing, he decided, was what kept him from rolling it back. The never-ending not knowing, and the unknowing. If he could say something. If he had the time. He could not let the world slip into that box. He could not let her slip into that box. He would not.

Arni pulled the covers off his body and felt his feet touch the cold floor. Spit the pill in the trash. Across the room, he pulled the door to the hallway open.

He had to wipe the water from his eyes to see. Had to steady his breathing. The light from the doorway reflected off Siggi's pupils. Drowsy, she raised a single finger to him. "*El... Els—*"

"Good night, *elskan mín*," he said, like every night, then closed the door and went back to work.

Feb. 11th, 2030

The ring.

Arni sat on the shore, looking out at the ocean. Where once the waves had crashed, there was now only a flat and dull expanse, all the way to the twinkling horizon. The air bit. It had taken fingers and toes. Still, he sat on the shore, because he had to.

"By the water again," he said. "Your favorite."

Thanks for reminding me, Arnar.

"Sorry," he said. He began again. "So I know we have, um, multiple layers of gloves on right now, but... think you can fit *this* on your finger?"

Awful. Not as charming as he thought.

"Can I show you something I've been saving?"

Too forward.

"Fuck. Fuck fuck fuck fuck FUCK!" He wound his arm back and hurled the damned thing into the ocean. It made a clink when it hit the ice, and skidded along until it came to a stop against a small crest, glinting diamond unmistakable.

There was a tight jolt in his chest. He forced the sob down. Tears came out, but crusted on contact with the air. He couldn't feel his cheeks, or his toes, or his fingers. Arni turned back towards the lights of the shelter, squat on the rocky plain. There always comes a time, *Mamma* had said, to go home. He took four steps in that direction.

But the ring was behind him. Sparkling there.

"Where did you go?" he whispered.

I think you kn—

"No. No. *No.*"

He rushed across the ice to grab it, but lost balance on the bad foot. He slipped once. Ran. Slipped again. With the three fingers of his left hand, he fumbled it into his right, then trudged back to the shore and found the same spot.

Arni took a deep breath.

"Siggi," he said. "Will you—"

It caught in his mouth.

Arni sat still for a while, rolling the ring between his fingers, eyes stuck on the horizon. He figured he'd get it before the sun rose.

See Damian Stockli's story "She Was the Universe" online at Metaphorosis.
If you liked it, leave a comment. Authors love that!
Remember to subscribe to our e-mail updates so you'll know when new stories are posted.

About the story

The first iteration of this story was written when I was 18, and dissatisfied with how human-centric alien invasion stories tend to be. I figured the only thing an interstellar civilization could want from us was the sun—making us the "ants in some nice-looking lumber"—and that idea stuck with me. The story's current form took shape during the height of the pandemic, where I revisited the idea for a Zoom class on writing about catastrophe. It reflects some of my own experience with loss and neurosis. In that way, you could probably frame it as a COVID story.

Some of the works in my head as I wrote it include the poem "Darkness", by Byron, which is where the title comes from; Ingmar Bergman's classic film The Seventh Seal; and a melodramatic pop song called "As the World Caves In" by Matt Maltese.

A question for the author

Q: How does writing speculative fiction affect your daily life?

A: I definitely don't think normally. My brain is always looking to relate some mundane observation to a gestalt, even when there is none. I'll hear a friend pronounce a word in an interesting way, and sixty seconds later I'm daydreaming about dialect variations in the NYC metro area. Then, at some point, I start speculating on fictional anthropologies. That leap is where the SF writer comes in, I suppose. My writing teachers always taught me to take notes on the world around me and use that in my writing. It's been good for making SF, but in my daily life it probably manifests mostly as inattentiveness.

About the author

Damian Stockli is a writer and graduate student from the Hudson Valley, in New York State. When he isn't doing thesis research on the grammatology of virtual semiotics, he's pursuing that childhood dream of writing a space opera—and all the short stories currently on deck. He hopes to finish them before age 30, or maybe 40.

damianstockli5.wordpress.com, @DamianStockli

The Antidote for Longing

Karl Dandenell

Part 3

Previously... Lars Bjornsen, the banished imperial poisoner, has returned to court in disguise, where he is reunited with his old friend, the imperial physik Fredrik Magnusson. Together, they investigate the mystery of Emperor Gustavus' illness and the apparent suicide of the newest imperial poisoner, Lord Anders. While the clues point to a possible coup attempt, Lars begins to suspect that Lord Anders has been feeding the emperor an aphrodisiac known as *Sweet Agony* to ensure a new heir. And for an old man like Emperor Gustavus, *Sweet Agony* can be a deadly poison.

I told Fredrik the story of the *Viktoria*, an imperial warship that patrolled the fjords around Oslo. Two score years ago, a strange sickness had struck *Viktoria*'s crew. Following an extended refit in Tønsberg, her sailors began sleeping through their shifts, and they repeatedly raided the captain's store of sweetmeats despite the heavy punishments meted out to restore discipline.

One boatswain and a cook, both of middle years, died without warning. Emil Krog, the imperial spymaster at that time, believed the tsar's agents had contaminated the ship's water barrels and called upon the Society to investigate. His suspicions proved false.

The Society eventually traced the crew's illness to a spiced wine served at the Lusty Mermaid bawdy house. When questioned, the owner admitted she'd hired an unscrupulous physik with the goal of 'fortifying the desires and increasing the flow of heart's blood' of her customers.

"The name *Sweet Agony* was said to have been coined as a salacious jest by the owner, but that part of the story is likely apocryphal," I said.

"An ingenious method to fatten one's purse," said Fredrik. "Still, why would Anders implement such a ploy, knowing it had killed several men?"

"We tested *Sweet Agony* and found it fatal only in extremely high doses. Very impractical, and thus, never formally adopted by the Society," I replied. "However, in repeated low doses, *Sweet Agony* increases fertility as well as desire."

"I hope that wasn't part of the Society's tests," said Fredrik.

"Oh no. The evidence came to light during an imperial tax audit of Tønsberg's orphanages," I said. "One of Gustavus's reforms provided a small stipend to women who surrendered their unwanted newborns."

Fredrik nodded. "It's certainly better than abandoning them to nature."

"But the audit found an unprecedented cluster of bastards appearing eight to nine months after the *Viktoria* left port. Turns out the Lusty Mermaid's girls contributed more than their usual share. Far more," I said and cleared my throat like a lecturer at the imperial academy. "Given all the evidence, I am confident we're dealing with nothing more than a simple overdose of *Sweet Agony*."

"Impressive deduction," said Fredrik and gently applauded.

His praise brought a flush to my cheeks. "This isn't my first encounter with *Sweet Agony*. Nor yours."

"What do you mean?"

"Do you remember the awful punch they served at the academy's Christmas parties?" I said.

"Gah," he said. "Half molasses and half *akvavit*. It did enliven the spirit, though."

"That's because the Society sells *Sweet Agony* to the senior students."

"That's terrible! Poisoning the best and brightest!"

"'Twas no more deadly than the *akvavit*. Besides, the profits go to the church." I tapped the cover of the novel next to me. "Anders is—was—a much younger man, so his memories of the academy were no doubt fresher. And this romance became his Mnemosyne."

I trimmed a quill and found a piece of foolscap. "Fortunately for His Majesty—and the rest of Europe—there is a simple counteragent." I inked my quill and commenced writing. "You'll need these herbs."

"Not anymore, no," agreed Fredrik. "You *were* very sick, though. So much so that I called in a trusted colleague for a consult. I'm sure he could explain it better than I." He glanced toward the screen. "Perhaps if Your Majesty feels up to it, I might arrange a brief visit."

I shook my head, even though Fredrik couldn't see me. An hour ago, before the emperor began to stir, Fredrik had suggested that we reveal my involvement in his recovery. I'd agreed, eager to seize this singular opportunity to regain his favor.

Now the plan struck me as foolhardy at best. The emperor's gratitude was a coin rarely spent, and certainly not wasted on men who failed him.

"Later, perhaps," said the emperor. "I'm starving. Have someone bring me food."

Fredrik rang the small bell on the side table. A moment later, the heavy oak door swung open and a servant entered.

"Some beef broth for His Majesty," said Fredrik.

"At once, my lord."

"And close the door behind you."

The servant bowed and departed, dragging the door closed with a solid thud.

"Help me sit up," said Gustavus. "I'm not an invalid to sup lying down."

"Of course." Fredrik arranged the feather pillows and refilled the emperor's cup. "Your Majesty, I have good news. Empress Anna is gravid."

"Finally. That woman was burning through the candle of my patience." He sipped more tea and grimaced. "Tastes like grass."

Two quick knocks announced a servant, who bore a silver tray with a matching bowl and spoon. He arranged the tray on the bed and stood at attention.

"Out," said the emperor, wielding his spoon with a steady hand. That, combined with his obvious energy, gave proof to the efficacy of the antidote. It was a small comfort and I clung to it.

"Gently, Your Majesty, gently. You haven't eaten for days."

Gustavus narrowed his eyes but set aside his spoon. "All right, Lord Physik. Tell me of the empress."

Fredrik's demeanor immediately brightened. "From all appearances she is quite healthy, and I anticipate no problems," he said. "Though it might be prudent if she were to return to Stockholm as soon as possible. Bed rest is normally called for, even though it's not her first child."

"Fine. See to it personally. I will join her after I have dealt with matters here."

"Yes, Majesty," said Fredrik. "And now that the poison is purged from your body, your usual vigor should return in short order."

Gustavus finished his soup. "Poison? Nonsense. Everything I eat and drink is inspected by Lord Anders or Lady Maja. Too many sweetmeats, that's all."

A braver man might have pushed aside the dressing screen and revealed the conspiracy, but my legs were weak. In that moment I was overwhelmed by my memories of Gustavus's anger when he'd learned of my blunder in Russia, and his swift order to banish me.

I crouched lower.

"Oh course, Your Majesty, of course," said Fredrik. "It's as you say, nothing more than overindulgence."

Gustavus closed his eyes. "Send for my chamberlain. I want a fresh dressing gown. And more food."

"Just some bread, if you please, Your Majesty."

"Yes, old hen. Bread. *And* butter. Now leave me."

Fredrik rose, bowed. "Yes, Your Majesty. I shall fetch the chamberlain."

When I emerged into the traveling library, two men were waiting for me, flintlocks pointed at my chest. "Hello, gentlemen," I said. "Oskar and Josef, if I remember correctly?"

"General," replied Oskar. He pressed a barrel to my forehead. Josef turned out my pockets, relieving me of poniard and flasks, then prodded me forward. "Downstairs, sir."

"I know the way," I said.

The dungeons at Strömsholm were much smaller than their counterparts in Stockholm, though no less disheartening. Chill dampness permeated everything. The Duke of Uppland's largess with demon lights did not extend this far below the castle; what little light there was came from lamps redolent of rancid whale oil. A tiny brazier burned desultorily beyond the iron gate of my cell and the thin blanket on the straw-covered pallet did little to soften it. I shook it out and wrapped myself, wishing for my great coat.

I sat and shivered, reviewing my mistakes. If I'd truly considered the risks involved, I might have hidden another weapon—or at least another flask—in my boot. If I'd been more alert, I might have heard Oskar and Josef in the library. Might have fled back into the secret passage. Might have disarmed one of the guards.

Might have made my escape.

It's particularly damning when the arc of your downfall is rooted in one clearly defined failure. Mine was Russia. If I'd successfully completed my mission then, I would mostly likely now be sitting by the fire upstairs with Fredrik, gently laughing over the ridiculous preparations for the emperor's upcoming fete. We might have had a game of chess, or a round of One and Thirty with the spymaster and the imperial machine mage, while dozens of functionaries kept the business of empire running smoothly around us.

But I hadn't succeeded in Russia. I'd been more concerned with getting home safely than with risking a second attempt. Now, my breath steamed in this frigid cell.

After a time, the corridor brightened with the warm light of a demon lamp. Maja Viklund entered the chamber, accompanied by my guards. Oskar hung the lamp from a rusty hook while Josef fetched a stool and placed it close to the cell's iron bars.

Maja turned her head slightly. "Wait outside." Then she perched on the stool.

I stood and doffed my hat. "Maja."

A flintlock appeared in her right hand. With her left, she gestured to the pallet. "General Bjornsen... have a seat."

She wore no rings or jewelry, nothing to indicate she was an influential member of court. Even her firearm was plain, with a patina of frequent use. Very unlike Birgitta's pistol. I lowered myself with deliberate slowness to my scratchy mattress, keeping a close eye on her finger as it floated above the trigger.

"You look well, Maja." She possessed a fierce beauty that still attracted me, even now.

"I am the same as I ever was, General... loyal," she said. "*You* however, appear very tired. Life in the country has... not agreed with you."

So it is to be titles and formality, I thought. *So be it.* "I never stopped being loyal, Spymaster. His Imperial Majesty needed me, so I am here."

She nodded. "You're loyal to your friends, at least. I didn't think the... imperial physik would be so bold as to contact you. Fortunately for me, Lieutenant Pernillasdotter understands her... duty. She has given me a full... accounting." After all these years, Maja still spoke as if she were just discovering the words. I remembered when I'd found the habit charming, like watching a child sounding out the pages of a storybook.

"Where's Lord Fredrik?" I said.

"My men are holding him in his chambers. I will have a conversation with him... presently." Her smile did not reach her eyes.

"Are these the same men who faked Lord Anders' suicide? Because they did a poor job of it."

She ignored my barb. "None of this would have been necessary if your successor had been more... cooperative. When His Majesty began nodding off at court, the imperial poisoner refused to... dose him any further."

"I presume that didn't stop you," I said.

"Indeed, Lord Anders left excellent notes. That and my own... training were sufficient to recreate the formula," she said. "I added the syrup to His Majesty's evening cordial, much like you did with Aleksey Mikhaylovich. Or rather... his mistress."

My faced burned with shame.

"But all that is... behind us now. The empire will soon have a proper heir, and nothing else matters, yes?" Maja pursed her lips. "It's a pity about Lord Anders, though. He was a raconteur, much like you... once were. I will inform... His Majesty that the young man fell into madness and took his own life. It... happens, does it not? All that time spent with poisons."

"I've seen it only once," I admitted. Which is why *Cracked Stone* is always prepared in a room with open windows.

"This may be another... such occurrence." She shrugged. The pistol didn't waver. "At the end of the day, I doubt the emperor will give the matter much thought. He has ... other concerns now. A birthday. A child."

I wanted to reach though the bars and seize her hand. Try to make her feel that connection we once had. But such impulsiveness would probably earn me a pistol ball and a quick trip to gallows for Fredrik. Instead, I focused on my words.

"His Majesty is an old man. He could have *died*."

"But he didn't," she said, matter-of-factly. "And even if he had, there are contingencies. Empress Anna and... a few well-chosen regents could guide the empire.

"My duty lies to the empire itself, General. Not the man. Everything and... everyone is secondary to that."

"I understand that now." The truth, so obvious now, pierced me. The woman I'd loved didn't understand honor. Perhaps that's why she'd never understood me?

"In the meantime... I find myself in need of a new imperial poisoner," she said. "Someone willing to do... what is necessary. Without question. Do you think the Society can direct me to such a... person?"

I hung my head, resigned to hear the price of my redemption. "I swear on my life I will protect Gustav Adolphus against his enemies and carry out his will," I said, repeating my Society oath.

"Good. There is value in... keeping oaths. Swear another one now. Swear to silence. You will never speak of this. Not to me. Not to anyone. Ever."

I swallowed against a dry throat. "I swear. Please, spare Lord Fredrik."

"I have no quarrel with him."

Relief flooded me. "What else do you want from me?"

"Nothing." She turned toward the corridor. "I'm finished here!"

The guards entered, pistols drawn. "Your carriage is waiting," Maja said, standing and tucking away her flintlock.

"Where am I going?"

"Home, General Bjornsen, where you belong. Home to your tea and your... peacocks."

"Wait! You said you need a new poisoner!" I hated the sudden desperation in my words. "I *saved* the emperor. I have earned the office."

"Yes, you certainly saved His Majesty from dyspepsia and... gout," she said. "I'm sure this will be taken into... consideration when the subject of your exile comes up. As far as an important court position is concerned..." She shrugged. "I have changed my mind. Good day." With a graceful incline of her head, she left.

I stood there for several minutes, eyes shut and fists clenched, fighting back tears, until Oskar cleared his throat. I stepped away from the cell door and he unlocked it.

I accompanied them through the castle, my back ramrod straight, eyes forward and lips clenched. They took me through the main gallery, the ballroom, and the reception hall. Though my escorts said nothing, there was a subtle shift in the genteel voices and gestures as we passed. A clear signal that I was unworthy of their rarefied company.

At least my silence will buy Fredrik's life. I held that thought close and prayed Maja would keep her word.

At the front gate stood an ordinary coach. Its frame and doors were painted a dull red most often associated with common houses and barns. This was the meanest sort of conveyance, something a yeoman secretary or *glädjeflicka* might hire on a rainy night.

Even the horses had dull eyes.

The driver, his head covered by a thick wool cap, climbed into his seat.

I shivered in the evening air and spoke for first time since leaving the dungeon. "May I have my coat?"

Josef snapped his fingers. Another footman stepped from the castle and handed over my great coat. I thanked him and clasped the familiar garment to my chest. "Your flask," said Josef. I turned.

He poured out most of its contents before tossing it to me. "The spymaster does not wish you to act rashly."

"Never again." I seated myself on the cold wooden bench. No demon jars or blankets to warm me here. The driver clucked his tongue. As the horses strained forward, the first tears came.

No one had offered the barest courtesy in farewell. No salute, no blessing, not even a tipping of their cap. They had dismissed me like a villain without rank or station.

I pulled the shades and inspected the great coat. The pockets were completely turned out and empty. My poniard was gone as well. Maja had apparently not wanted me to open a vein, at least not until I arrived home.

With shaking fingers, I opened my flask and drank the remaining drops. As the *Dream Caller* took effect, I vowed I would someday devise an antidote to purge my heart of this longing and loneliness.

I woke to the mocking calls of peacocks.

*See Karl Dandenell's story "The Antidote for Longing III"
online at Metaphorosis.
If you liked it, leave a comment. Authors love that!
Remember to subscribe to our e-mail updates so you'll
know when new stories are posted.*

Copyright

Title information

Metaphorosis September 2023

ISSN: 2573-136X (online)
ISBN: 978-1-64076-265-7 (e-book)
ISBN: 978-1-64076-266-4 (paperback)

Copyright

Works of fiction

This book contains works of fiction. Characters, dialogue, places, organizations, incidents, and events portrayed in the works are fictional and are products of the author's imagination or used fictitiously. Any resemblance to actual persons, places, organizations, or events is coincidental.

All rights reserved

Moral rights asserted

Each author whose work is included in this book has asserted their moral rights, including the right to be identified as the author of their respective work(s).

Publisher

Metaphorosis

a magazine of speculative fiction

Metaphorosis Magazine is an imprint of
Metaphorosis Publishing
Neskowin, OR, USA

www.metaphorosis.com

"Metaphorosis" is a registered trademark.

Discounts available

Substantial discounts are available for educational institutions, including writing workshops. Discounts are also available for quantity purchases. For details, contact Metaphorosis at metaphorosis.com/about

Metaphorosis Publishing

Metaphorosis offers beautifully written science fiction and fantasy. Our imprints include:

Metaphorosis Magazine
Plant Based Press
Verdage
Vestige

You can also find us:
Metaphorosis@writing.exchange
@Metaphorosis
www.facebook.com/metaphorosis

Help keep Metaphorosis running by supporting us at
Patreon.com/metaphorosis

See more about some of our books on the following pages.

Metaphorosis Magazine

Metaphorosis is an online speculative fiction magazine dedicated to quality writing. We publish an original story every week, along with author bios, interviews, and notes on story origins.

We also publish monthly print and e-book issues, as well as yearly Best of and Complete anthologies.

Come and see us online at magazine.Metaphorosis.com.

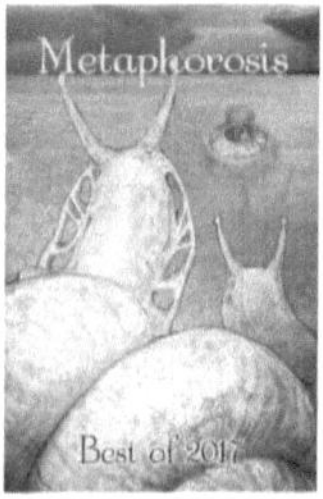

Plant Based Press

plant
based
press

Vegan-friendly science fiction and fantasy, including anthologies of the year's best SFF stories, from 2016-2020.

Chambers of the Heart
speculative stories
by
B. Morris Allen

A heart that's a building, a dog that's a program, a woman sinking irretrievably — stories about love, loss, and motion.

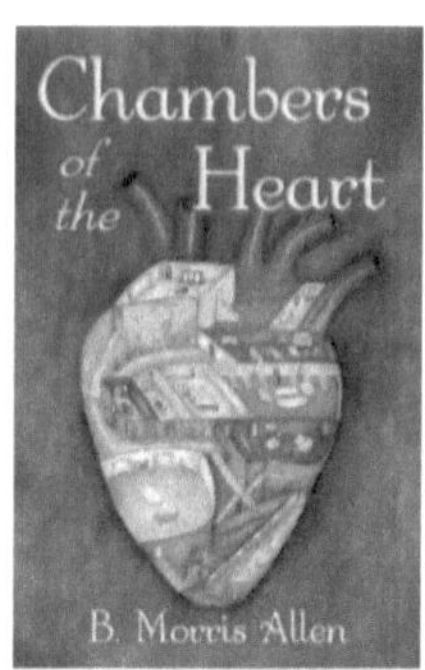

Susurrus

A darkly romantic story of magic, love, and suffering.

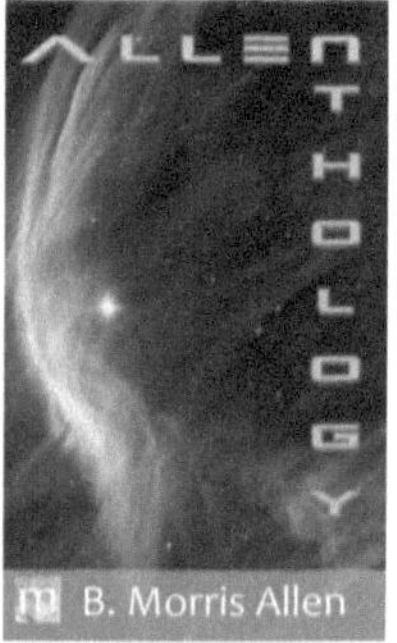

Allenthology: Volume I

Including three full collections of SFF stories.

Verdage

Verdage

Science fiction and fantasy books for writers — full of great stories, often with an additional focus on the craft of speculative fiction writing.

Reading 5X5 x3

Changes

How do stories move from 'maybe' to published?

Here are 15 case studies of stories published in *Metaphorosis* magazine.

Reading 5X5 x2

Duets

How do authors' voices change when they collaborate?

A round-robin of five talented science fiction and fantasy authors collaborating with each other and writing solo.

Including stories by Evan Marcroft, David Gallay, J. Tynan Burke, L'Erin Ogle, and Douglas Anstruther.

Score

an SFF symphony

An anthology with an emotional score from the heights of joy to the depths of despair – but always with a little hope shining through.

Reading 5X5

Five stories, five times

See how different
writers take on
the same material.

Reading 5X5

Writers' Edition

Two extra stories,
the story seed,
and authors' notes
on writing.

Vestige

Novelettes, novellas, and novels by Metaphorosis authors.

The Nocturnals
Mariah Montoya

Night is Dangerous. Day is deadly.

Where day and night last thirty years, humans move constantly stay ahead of the night and cruel Nocturnals that call it home. But a boy is lost out there.

Joyful Heave

Science fiction and fantasy anthologies with innovative and unusual themes.

Museum Piece
an unusual collection

A gallery of the strange and outrageous

Step right up and enter a world of wonder and oddities! These museums are not your typical tourist traps. From the Museum of Lost Dreams to the Suicide Museum, each exhibit will take you on a journey you won't soon forget.